Sealing Fate

Sealing Fate

A novel of passion, human frailty and obsession.

David P. Warren

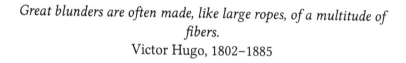

Great blunders are often made, like large ropes, of a multitude of fibers.
Victor Hugo, 1802–1885

To Nancy, Melissa, Marc, and Eric, for love and inspiration are inseparable.

Chapter 1

Speaker of the House Sean Gilmore shook Brian's hand and smiled at him approvingly. "Congratulations, my boy. You've really done it. Welcome to the world of politics."

The comment was condescending, and on any other night, it might have been offensive. But not tonight. Tonight, even the glib and ingenuous Gilmore couldn't offend Brian. It was his night. And this was California's senior congressman welcoming the newest member of the House of Representatives to the fold.

Brian nodded at Gilmore, and the photographers who had made the select list snapped their cameras repeatedly. Brian had been told often enough that he photographed well. At thirty-seven, his thick brown hair held off all traces of gray. His wide brown eyes gave off a sparkle that he joked was confusion often mistaken for intelligence. Brian's self-deprecating humor was always well received. It made a rising star just one of the gang. The slight dimple when Brian smiled completed the salable political image. He was packaged as some combination of John Kennedy and Jimmy Stewart.

As they stood together to be photographed, Brian and Gilmore presented an obvious contrast in gene pools. Gilmore was almost bald, but refusing to concede the point, he arranged his last few strands of hair across the dome of his head, ear to ear. His wry smile suggested he had a secret. Brian suspected he had many. Gilmore was grossly overweight since his levels of exercise did not keep pace with years of catered events like this one.

Gilmore turned to the guests who had packed the banquet room of his mansion and raised his glass. "May I have your attention, ladies and gentlemen?" He waited with a dignified smile as the room became quiet. "I'd like to make a toast to the beginning of a great political career." Then he turned toward Brian. "And I'd like to welcome Brian Madsen to the party stronghold." He thrust his glass toward the black-tie crowd and held the pose.

Gilmore was always posing. After twenty-five years in politics, Brian doubted he could stop. But the son of a bitch did have flare. Glasses were raised, and cheers rang out across the expansive room. White-coated servers scurried around to refill glasses before they emptied.

"There is no limit to what we can accomplish together." He threw his arm around Brian, and flashes went off around the room.

As Gilmore moved into the crowd to mingle, Brian surveyed the room. Speaker Gilmore had lent more than his opulent Beverly Hills mansion to the occasion. His influence was evident in the guest list. The movers and shakers of politics, a healthy share of *Fortune* 500 executives, and the who's who of Hollywood were all present to pay tribute to Brian. Big money filled the place. Many had contributed to the campaign to get Brian elected once the party had gotten behind him, and the rest would now. Doors were open. Staggering power and influence was in this room, all now available to Brian. He was the candidate of the power brokers around him who would love to do him favors: raising money, gaining access to the most exclusive of clubs, or whatever he wanted.

"Congratulations, Brian." The deep voice came from a rotund man with a thick beard but little hair on his head.

"Thank you, Jim. I'm delighted you came." Brian shook the hand of James Francis Orson, former secretary of state and attendant to three past presidents. Now to Brian, he was just Jim.

"I wouldn't have missed it for the world. You're the right man for the job. Whatever assistance I can lend, call me. I still know how to get a number of things done in Washington."

Brian knew what an understatement that was. Orson could get a new bill onto the floor of either house or swing a close vote. He could arrange an audience with the president if he so desired.

"It's gratifying to have your support, Jim. I may take you up on that offer." Brian shook hands with Orson once more before moving on to a circle of well-wishers.

Brian's champagne glass was refilled between brief visits with dignitaries as he moved from group to group. It was eleven o'clock before he had a moment to himself. He looked around the room. The crowd wasn't thinning and wouldn't for hours.

From his left, Brian heard a familiar voice. "Quite a night, isn't it, man of the hour?" Barbara kissed him on the cheek.

He turned toward her. Her layered black hair was perched royally on her shoulders, flipping upward. Her green eyes, high cheekbones, and soft smile worked together to convey good breeding. Her movements were graceful elegance. She was the girl most of the boys in high school were attracted to but were sure they couldn't get.

"Quite a night," she repeated, glancing around the room.

"It's just incredible." Brian smiled.

"Well, this is your night."

"It's all so hard to believe."

She smiled warmly. "Nothing that a brilliant mind can't achieve on the heels of a dozen years with the most successful law firm in the state and eight years of local politics."

"This is a long way from the unnoticed city council meetings we used to do. Having influential clients didn't hurt either." He kissed Barbara's cheek. "And having a beautiful and supportive wife."

She grinned at him. "See, you're already a politician. You earned it, Brian. Bask in it." She saw a familiar face across the room. "See you later, Congressman. I'm going to mingle."

Brian watched her walk away. She was the perfect Congressman's wife—attractive, charming, and intelligent. As he watched her greet an elderly couple, he felt a sense of loss. He thought back to the first days of their marriage in the small apartment they could barely afford. They had been so close.

Somewhere along the way, our lives together had become a business. Had it been a necessary cost of growing a political career, or did I get my priorities confused? Or was there a difference? Brian acknowledged a feeling of loss as he swirled the remnants of his third glass of champagne.

Another voice broke into his thoughts. "You make a dashing congressman, you know?"

Brian smiled and turned to see Cathy Jenkins smiling at him. She wore a black strapless dress and a single strand of pearls. Her blonde hair cascaded down over her shoulders and accentuated the blueness of her eyes.

He gave her a hug. "We did it, didn't we?"

She smiled. "*You* did it. I'm just one of the support staff."

Brian shook his head. "Not so. The whole team made this possible."

He had seen Cathy frequently at campaign headquarters. She had worked hard for his election, but he wasn't sure why. All he really knew about her was that she worked for International Resource Corporation and she always had a smile for him.

"This is your night, Brian."

He looked into wide blue eyes that seemed to invite him in. "I don't think we've ever had more than five minutes to talk. Seems like you know a lot more about me than I do about you."

"The price of being a rising star." Those eyes sparkled. She looked around the room at the visiting elite. "This is a night you'll remember for some time."

Brian smiled and nodded. "It is a wonderful night for all of us." He looked down at the empty glass she held. "Can I get you a drink?"

Cathy looked down at the glass and then back at him. She said nothing. Her blue eyes became liquid as she stared deeply into Brian's brown eyes. He found himself lost in those eyes. Time was passing, but he wasn't sure how much. He was no longer aware of the others in the room.

"Come with me," Cathy said in a whisper. She took his hand and led him from the banquet room.

A tall, mustached man watched them from across the room. The man was in his fifties, but his youthful, elegant features, salt-and-pepper hair, and black tuxedo made him appear to have just stepped from the cover of *GQ*. He was not a celebrity who had been squeezed into the attire to conform to the *GQ* mold but an unknown who looked the part naturally. The man stood in a circle of others befitting his image, no longer listening to the conversation. His thoughts strayed to the guest of honor and his attractive companion. She was familiar to him. He had seen her around the company, but he couldn't place her.

He watched them walk from the room. He wasn't sure why, but on impulse, he decided to follow. He excused himself and slowly moved toward the door. The man watched as Cathy led Brian up the stairs. He waited several seconds before following at a safe distance.

Brian and Cathy walked down the marbled hall to the stair-case and began to climb to the second floor.

"Where are we going?" Brian's voice was slightly cracking.

"I'll show you."

At the top of the stairs, she pulled him down the wide cor-ridor, past nineteenth-century tables, priceless sculptures, and expressionless, expressionist paintings. She opened the second door on the right and pulled Brian inside. It was a large bathroom.

Cathy walked back to the door, gave the lock in the door handle a twist, and turned to look at Brian. A grin came over her face, and she walked toward him. "I just wanted the opportunity to congratulate you privately." She put her arms around his neck. "Damn good work, Brian. You'll do very well."

"Thanks. You were a great help to me, you know? I really appreciate all you've done."

"Really?" She leaned back to look into his eyes.

"Of course. You gave—-"

Cathy pulled Brian toward her and kissed him softly. He didn't resist. Maybe it was the champagne. Perhaps it was her. He found himself kissing back. He recognized a longing for this woman he barely knew. The kiss intensified. Their mouths opened, and their hands began to grope.

Brian placed a hand on her breast. She leaned toward him. His hand slid down her side and lifted her dress. He ran his hand up her leg. Nothing was under the dress. He felt her groping at his belt and then his zipper. His pants fell to the floor. She sat on the counter and wrapped her legs around him. He felt the moisture. Then he was inside her. Her arms were under his shirt.

As the thrusts grew in intensity, her nails cut into his back. Brian could hear her moaning louder and louder. He could feel himself inside her, ready to explode. The rest of the world was gone. Cathy cried out, louder with each thrust. Brian suppressed the sounds with his mouth on hers.

She arched her back for the final thrusts, and Brian pulled her toward him. He held her tightly as the release came. Moans filled the room. He looked into those blue eyes and saw a contented smile.

Reality suddenly came back to him. Instinctively, Brian looked around. He suddenly realized that the bathroom door was ajar, and it seemed to move slightly. Brian pulled up his pants and held them at his waist. He ran to the door. It was open just enough to allow him to glimpse a small portion of the hall. He could see nothing. He touched the door handle, and it wouldn't turn. It was still in the locked position.

Brian opened the door little by little until he could see the entire hallway. There was no one. He sighed with relief as he realized that the door must have been locked, but not completely closed.

He buttoned his pants as he walked over to Cathy and told her, "Everything's okay."

She gave him a radiant smile. Brian knew he would feel guilty later. Right now, he had to get back to the party before he was missed … before it was known that they were missing together.

Cathy kissed him on the cheek. "That was wonderful, Congressman." She straightened her dress and her hair. Then she checked her makeup. "I'll go back first."

He nodded and then smiled. "That really was wonderful."

She grinned back and walked out the door. "See you soon."

As he walked down the stairs, the noise of the party grew louder. Everything seemed to be just as he had left it. He checked his watch. Almost twenty minutes had passed. He looked around and saw Barbara standing with three women on the other side of the room. She waved to him, smiling. He waved back.

Brian expected that guilt would soon overcome him. He had never cheated on Barbara in their ten years together. All that had suddenly changed in twenty minutes. He knew there would be a price to pay. But so far, the feelings were only good. He thought of Cathy's moans and smiled. He could see it all in his head, and he could still feel himself inside her.

Brian excused himself from a group of bank industry executives, shaking hands with each one more time as they offered congratulations. He took a moment to look around the room. It had been over two hours since he returned from his encounter with Cathy, and nothing was out of order. It was like the affair had never happened. This was still his night.

Brian spotted Barbara talking to a man with salt-and-pepper hair and made his way toward them.

As he walked up to him, the man turned to him and smiled. "Congratulations, Congressman," he said, offering Brian his hand.

Brian shook the hand. "Thank you," he said appreciatively.

The man looked at his watch. "I've really got to be going." He slapped Brian on the arm. "Quite a night to remember. Congratulations to both of you." He turned and gave them a wave as he moved away.

Barbara returned the wave and then turned to Brian. "Sorry about that. I would have introduced you, but if I ever knew who that was, I've since forgotten."

Brian shrugged. "Don't worry. It's not like he's the only one I don't know. I can't keep track of half of these people." He gestured to the thinning crowd in the room. He chuckled and then said, "It's after two o'clock. How about we get out of here?"

Barbara nodded. "Sounds good. I'm running out of gas."

Brian and Barbara said goodnight to Speaker Gilmore, who struck a final pose for the last of the photographers at the door. They drove home in silence, each lost in thoughts of the evening. When they arrived home, they got ready for bed. Barbara took off her makeup while Brian prepared coffee for the morning. They met back in the bedroom and climbed into bed.

Barbara kissed him. "Congratulations, Congressman. I'm proud of you." She touched his cheek as they faced each other in bed. "I love you."

Brian kissed her softly. "I love you too."

He was still waiting for the guilt. Brian drifted off to sleep easily and dreamed of making love to a beautiful woman. He couldn't see the face of his partner, and in the morning when he awoke, he wondered if he had been dreaming of Barbara or Cathy.

Chapter 2

The next morning, Barbara made French toast and coffee. She and Brian sat in the dining area, looking out the bay window at the expanse of lawn in the backyard. There were birds in the trees, seeming to float effortlessly from one to another. Their sounds filled the air in a chorus of unrehearsed harmony.

Barbara was in a great mood, still intoxicated by the celebration they had shared the night before. She kissed Brian sweetly as she walked from the table to the stove. "So how does it feel to wake up a congressman?"

Brian smiled as he set down his coffee cup. "It feels pretty damn good. Still a little hard to believe, but good."

She nodded. "Well, I can't think of anyone who deserves the success more." Barbara walked over to Brian and rubbed his shoulders. "What's the timetable before session begins?"

"I've got three weeks here to find offices, get local staff in line, and start getting caught up on legislation that's up for vote. Then it'll be time to set up in Washington before session begins."

She kissed him on the cheek. "You'll let me know what I can do to help."

"Yes, I will." He took a sip of coffee. "I think we may have a lot of entertaining to do over the next few weeks."

"More mingling with the power merchants, huh?"

"Yeah, I'm afraid it goes with the job."

She shrugged after a moment. "That's okay. I enjoy meeting all these high rollers."

Everything was still going Brian's way. He had only good thoughts about last night. He had made love to a relative stranger while two hundred people waited downstairs. It was way out of character. It was something he would have condemned. But he remembered it with a smile, and there was still no guilt. For the first time, he thought his little indiscretion might just go undiscovered and unpunished. Brian smiled at Barbara and then pulled her close and kissed her.

Over the next few days, Brian found himself thinking of Cathy often. He had heard about groupies and star-fuckers, women who wanted to sleep with movie stars, rock stars, or Congressmen, just to do it. Brian felt sure that she was not one of them, but he really knew nothing about her or her motives. It also occurred to him that he had made himself vulnerable to her.

Now Cathy had something on him that could end his career before it got off the ground. Brian wasn't sure why, but he wasn't worried. He was sure that she wasn't a blackmailer. And he wanted to see her again, to talk to her and to tell her how good it had been.

Maybe even to make love with her again, he thought.

On Wednesday, Brian was working hard at getting resources aligned for the session. Two newly hired staff assistants and a secretary occupied the makeshift offices that had been his campaign headquarters. He spent most of his day on the telephone. Brian was finding his way around Washington, as best he could, by telephone. Seasoned Congressmen were anxious to meet him to enlist his support for pet projects.

Brian concluded a conversation Speaker Gilmore had initiated to seek his support for a tax reduction bill by saying he would give it serious study. He knew he would not support the bill but wanted time to reflect on how to tell Gilmore without creating a significant rift in the newly united party.

Brian put down the telephone and rubbed his eyes. The feel of Cathy's body came to him suddenly. He could feel her legs wrapped around him. He looked up, and she was standing in the doorway.

"Knock, knock," Cathy said. "May I come in?"

"Please." Brian stood quickly and walked over to meet her. "Please do."

She was wearing jeans and a blue top. Brian realized she looked great casual too.

She sat down in a visitor's chair and smiled. "How's the new job so far?"

Brian sat behind his desk and shook his head. "It'll take me a while to adjust, but so far, so good."

She fastened those blue eyes on him. "I've thought a lot about our time together over the weekend," she said in a serious tone.

"Yes, I have too," Brian said.

"Really?" She was quiet for a moment, looking down at her lap and then back at him. "I want you to know that, what happened last weekend, it's not something I do. I mean, I've never done anything like that before."

Brian nodded. He thought about George Orwell's *1984*, how Winston had smiled at the fact that his lover had done it before and done it often and that she had frequently enjoyed the forbidden fruit of passion in defiance of a society that forbade it. Brian wanted just the opposite. He wanted it to be unique and special to her. He was glad their passion had meant something to Cathy too.

"I think I knew that," he said softly.

"I hoped so. I'm not some kind of political groupie or something. I've just ... " The thought trailed off while she searched for words. "Truthfully I've been attracted to you since the first day I saw you in the campaign office. I mean, I volunteered because I thought you were the right man for the job. But after I met you, the motivation was more personal."

She shrugged. "Anyway, I've been thinking about you this week, and it was just important to me that you know I've never done that before and that you're special. That's all." She smiled at him and then stood up and turned to leave. "I hope to see you again soon, Brian."

He stopped her before she got to the door. "Cathy."

She turned and looked at him.

"How about tonight?" he asked. "I'll be out of here at about six. How about dinner?"

She didn't answer.

"I've been thinking about you too. I wanted to see you again," Brian said, almost pleading.

She nodded finally. "All right. Where?"

"O'Reilly's on Bridge Street."

"I'll be there." She turned and left the room.

Brian had trouble keeping his thoughts on his work for the rest of the afternoon. He knew the odds of something going wrong—-of getting caught—were increasing exponentially if he saw Cathy again. He knew of the risks to his career and his marriage. But he couldn't get her out of his mind. He had to see her again. There was really no choice.

At seven o'clock, Brian and Cathy sat at a corner table in O'Reilly's surrounded by plants and wood paneling. The soft lighting applied shadowy highlights to her sensuous lips. Brian told himself he was going off the deep end. He wasn't a compulsive man, but she had a hold on him. He had called Barbara at five thirty and told her he would be working late, meeting and greeting his constituents.

"It's good to see you," Cathy said, pulling Brian out of his thoughts.

He raised his bourbon; she hoisted her white wine. She wore a blue print dress with shoulder straps. It was not revealing, but it accentuated her shapely form. Her blonde hair flowed over a matching blue hair band, framing those consuming blue eyes.

"You look lovely tonight."

She smiled. Then her expression turned serious. "I thought about calling you and canceling several times this afternoon."

He held his breath and waited as her expression was suddenly serious.

"I'm not sure where all this will lead us," she said after a moment.

He nodded. "I'm not either, but I wanted to see you again. I've had you on my mind a lot."

They were silent while the waiter brought their meals. "Anything else, sir?"

Brian looked over at Cathy, and she shook her head. "No, I think we're fine. Thanks."

"Very well, sir," the man said and quickly disappeared.

Brian looked at his shrimp scampi. The meal looked fine, but he suddenly had no appetite. He picked at the meal and then looked up at Cathy to find her observing him.

"I'm not real hungry either," she said, having watched him play with his food for a while.

Brian put down his fork. "I thought I was ready to eat but ..." He shrugged. "I think I'm just a little too excited by the occasion."

Cathy smiled and leaned toward him. "You are?"

Brian raised his eyebrows in a gesture that said, "And how."

"Oh yeah. All my organs are upside down, and I'm manufacturing enough stomach acid to eat through my shirt anytime now."

She wrinkled her face. "Nice image. The stomach that ate Bridge Street."

Brian laughed. "Just symptoms."

She regarded him curiously. "Symptoms of what?"

He grinned widely. "Chemistry. Damn good chemistry."

The waiter came by and stared down at the dishes in astonishment. His expression suggested some tragedy had suddenly befallen him. "Is there something wrong with your meals, sir?" He turned to look at Cathy. "Ma'am?"

"No, there's nothing wrong," Brian reassured the man. "The food is fine. Turns out we're just not as hungry as we thought we were.

The waiter's serious expression remained. "I understand, sir. Can I take your dishes?"

He looked at Cathy, who nodded. "Yes, I think we're finished."

"Will there be anything else tonight, sir?" the waiter asked, getting on with business.

"No, that's all. Thanks." Brian handed the man a credit card.

When the waiter returned, Brian signed the receipt and thanked the man again to ease any distress caused by the un-eaten food. He helped Cathy into her coat, and they left the restaurant and walked toward the parking lot.

"What now?" she asked.

"Can I see you home?"

She smiled at him. "I should say no." She paused and seemed to be pondering something. "But then again, I shouldn't be here."

Brian kissed her softly on the forehead. "I'm glad you are."

She looked up at him and smiled warmly. He saw concession in those blue eyes. "Come on. I'll show you my apartment," she said, taking his hand.

They walked to her car. He kissed her softly on the lips and walked to his car. Ten minutes later, they parked beneath the apartment building, and she showed him to the elevator to her apartment.

He looked around her apartment, discovering more about her as he did. The decor was elegant but homey. There was a Thomas Kinkade picture of a lover's cottage by a stream. There was a conversation grouping of chairs, separated from the fire-place by an ornate throw rug. Brian followed Cathy into the kitchen, a broad expanse of blue tiled countertops and oak cupboards. Brian saw a breakfast nook with a window that looked out onto an atrium.

"What can I get you?" she asked.

Brian took her hand. "Just the pleasure of your company." He thought about how corny that sounded.

She smiled at him though. They walked into the living room, and Cathy lit a fire. Then she sat next to Brian to watch its flames dance, tossing sparks upward and casting moving shadows.

"So tell me more about you. What do you do for International Resources?" Brian asked.

"I didn't know you remembered I worked there," she said with a surprised look.

"I'm remembering everything I can about you. And I want to know more."

"I run the marketing department of the health care division. I package medical plans to sell to companies. We find ways to make HMOs appealing. Then we sell them to other corporations. We also market our hospitals and medical centers to businesses directly. We try to get companies to send their people to our doctors." She paused and wrinkled her brow. "I sound like a commercial."

Brian grinned. "How many hospitals and medical centers does the company have?"

"A lot; at last count, two hundred and six. There may be more by the end of the week."

"I had no idea the medical division of International was that big."

"Every division is that big. It's amazing. That's why I get a staff of twelve in marketing."

"What do you like to do when you're not working?" he asked.

"Oh, the hobbies question. Well, I like movies, playing tennis, and reading." She paused and then smiled. "And lately, thinking about you."

Brian stood and extended his hand. She took his hand, and he gently pulled her to her feet.

"I want you to know that I've never done this either," he said. "But I really want to be with you." He kissed Cathy passionately and felt the fire next to him and within him.

She closed her eyes and held him tightly. Slowly he undid the buttons on her blouse. She stepped out of her skirt and then began to undress him. On the ornate rug in front of the fire, they made love for the second time. The fire, the room, and the world disappeared. There was only the two of them becoming one and holding the moment as long as they could.

It was midnight when Brian returned home. Barbara didn't ask him any questions, but there was something there, something uncomfortable that hung in the air. When they had coffee the next morning, it was still there. She was quietly watching and examining. Brian could sense something unspoken. It was still there when he left for work.

Chapter 3

The executive offices of International Resource Corporation were elegant. They swallowed up the thirtieth through thirty-fifth floors of the Eastern Bank building. The thirty-fifth floor was known to the rest of the corporation as "Upstairs." It housed five senior vice presidents and, at its innermost sanctum, two executive vice presidents and the president.

In one of the three office suites of the inner sanctum, Michael Hayward stood staring out the window at the afternoon skyline. Evening traffic that didn't move jammed the streets. Pedestrians ran in seemingly random directions, making their way to their cars to further the congestion. He moved his eyes upward, and his reflection smiled back at him.

His salt-and-pepper hair and mature good looks would soon be featured in the business section of the *Times*. Next week would be the announcement. Jackson F. Parker was retiring after thirty-two years, and the presidency would belong to Michael or Jason Ross. The two executive vice presidents had been going head to head in the campaign for the position for more than six months. They had attempted to outdo one another with revenues and profits within their divisions. They had worked on Parker, who would name his own successor privately and in board meetings, and now the time was at hand.

Michael turned from the window and sat at his large mahogany desk. He couldn't help smiling when he thought about it. The empire was almost his. His acquisition of Telstar Corporation last year and its subsequent breakup and resale at a three hundred million-dollar profit this year had locked it in. He was still being congratulated. Next week it would be official.

Within thirty days, he would be occupying the president's office, not that he needed the extra office space. His office was thirty feet long and twenty-five feet wide. One wall was dedicated to a cherry wood bookcase. Another was all glass, floor to ceiling. The remaining two walls housed a full bar and stereo system and a variety of awards, clippings, and souvenirs reflecting the many acquisitions Michael had been involved in over the years. There was a circular conference table and five leather chairs in one corner of the office. Toward the center of the room was a conversation grouping, made up of a black leather couch and oversized black leather chair that faced each other, separated by a cherry wood coffee table.

Michael's office was adjoined by a large private conference room. Out front, his secretary occupied a room of almost equal size. The office of the president would give him a fireplace, a second conference room, and a full bathroom, nothing that Michael cared about. What he wanted was the power, total control of the company and total control of Jason Ross. And once that bitter rivalry had ended, Michael would keep Ross in charge of one of the smaller divisions. He would be a good man once he did what he was told.

There was a buzz. Michael picked up the telephone. "Yes, Sheila."

"Your wife is on line two," the friendly voice of his secretary said.

"Thanks. And get me the files on the Insignia Insurance acquisition, will you?"

"Yes, sir."

Michael pushed a button on the phone. "Hi, Carol."

Carol spoke in soft, tentative tones that sounded apologetic for the interruption. "Just wanted to let you know I'm going to Janet's for our regular Wednesday night dinner together. What time are you coming home tonight?"

"Probably late. I've got an eight thirty meeting. It'll be eleven or so when I get home."

"All right. I'll be home by then."

"Okay, bye."

"Bye."

Michael put down the telephone and thought about Carol. He wondered if she ever had affairs with all the free time she had. They hadn't been close in a number of years, but he had never learned of her having any involvement with another man. Either she still didn't fool around or she was very discreet. Michael smiled wryly. It was more a curiosity than a concern. It really didn't much matter, as long as Carol kept a low profile.

Sheila walked in with three thick files and put them on the conference table at the far side of the office. She was an attractive woman of about thirty-five with blonde hair pulled straight back and clipped at the base of her neck.

"Here's Insignia," she said.

Michael nodded.

"You must be pretty excited." A grin appeared on her face.

"There's nothing official yet," Michael said, trying not to return the smile.

"Yeah, but there's no doubt. There's no way they'll give it to Jason Ross after the deals you've done in the last few years. Everybody knows it's going to be you. The whole executive office is buzzing about it, talking about what kind of restructuring you're going to do, who's in and who's not. That kind of stuff."

Michael's smile broke free now. "You ready to be executive assistant to the president?"

"I've been ready ever since I heard Parker was retiring. See you later." Sheila turned and walked out the door.

Michael checked his watch. It was six thirty. He walked over to the wet bar and fixed himself a bourbon. Before opening the Insignia files, he stood at the window and toasted the city, the company, and his imminent appointment as its leader.

* * *

At seven, Brian completed his conference call with Congressman Howell and his assistant. His staff of two had just gone home for the day. Brian looked across the office at Barbara. She sat in a visitor's chair waiting for him. She had been lingering there for about twenty minutes. The phone light flashed again.

Brian gestured with a hand across his brow. "Almost done. Just this one last call."

Barbara nodded. "It's all right. I understand." She held her coat on her lap and watched him pick up the phone.

He punched the flashing button. "Hello, Brian Madsen here."

Brian flinched and then looked in Barbara's direction. He listened for a few moments and then said, "Okay, Thursday at ten o'clock. See you then." He put down the telephone and looked at Barbara. "Let's go have dinner. I want to get out of here before anything else happens." Brian walked over to her and kissed her lightly on the cheek.

She smiled, threw her arms around him, and kissed him full on the lips. "I've missed you, Mr. Congressman. Let's spend some time together."

Brian smiled tightly back at her. She put her arm around his waist, and they walked out of the office together, Brian hitting the light switch and locking the door as they left.

* * *

On Thursday morning, Michael Hayward saw the blonde woman walking through the building lobby. He stopped and watched her. It was definitely her; the woman he had seen sneak away with the new Congressman. Michael thought back to following them up the stairs and down the hall and to what he had seen when he slowly opened the bathroom door. He was sure they had never seen him watching.

On impulse, Michael walked away from the executive elevator bank and across the lobby to a bank of elevators for floors twenty to thirty-five. The doors to one of the elevators opened, and people poured inside. It was almost full when Michael climbed aboard. He wasn't far from her, but she appeared to be deep in thought and didn't look in his direction. The elevator stopped at the twentieth floor, and a few people got off. Three more unloaded at twenty-three and then two at twenty-five. The crowds were thinning.

At twenty-eight, she and one other woman got off. Michael followed a few feet behind her, trying not to be noticed. He knew the twenty-eighth floor was marketing and advertising.

He followed at a safe distance as she walked down one of the corridors, turning left onto another. Then she disappeared into an office. From there, it didn't take Michael long to determine who she was, Catherine Jenkins, marketing director. He didn't approach her. Michael didn't even know why he had followed her, other than curiosity about the sensuous woman he had seen making love to another man at a party. Michael turned and walked back toward the elevator banks.

A secretary in a green print dress watched him walk away. "Jenny, isn't that Michael Hayward?"

The secretary at the adjacent desk stood to get a better view of him disappearing down the hall. "The next president?"

"Yeah. I think that was him."

"Maybe, but the penthouse guys don't usually show up on this floor."

The secretary in the green print nodded. "I know. I felt like trying to get an autograph."

At ten o'clock on Thursday morning, Brian sat in Josie's Coffee Shop, staring at the door and waiting. Pink booths lined the window that looked out on the street. The booths also occupied the adjoining wall, forming an L-shape that surrounded the black, circular swivel seats that lined the counter. Josie's was a favorite of the locals, where good food was inexpensive and the relaxation was easy.

Cathy came in and looked around until she saw him waving in her direction. A warm smile came to her face, and she walked over to him and kissed his cheek before sitting across from him in the booth. She wore a gray suit with a red blouse. Her hair was up, which made her look taller. Brian noticed how big her blue eyes looked. She was mesmerizing.

"Good morning, Congressman," she said sweetly.

"Good morning," he replied, unable to take his eyes from her face.

A female server was beside the table immediately. "What can I get you?"

"Some coffee would be good," Cathy said.

The server nodded and turned to go.

"Good to see you," Cathy said to Brian, taking his hand across the table.

"You too. You look great."

"Thanks. But I bet you say that to all the marketing directors who want to screw your brains out."

Brian stifled a laugh. "One for one so far."

"I'm glad you had time to get together this morning. I just didn't want to wait until tomorrow night to see you again."

"Me either."

"Come with me," she said, standing up. "I want to show you something."

The server placed a cup of coffee in front of where Cathy. "You change your mind?"

"Maybe," Cathy said.

She put five dollars on the table and took Brian by the hand, leading him out of the restaurant and into the parking lot. She stopped in front of a Mustang convertible. "What do you think?"

"New car?" he asked.

"Yeah." She kissed him on the cheek. "Take a ride with me."

Brian looked at his watch. "I don't know if we should right—-"

"Get in."

Cathy climbed behind the wheel, and Brian got into the passenger seat. She put the top down, and they headed out of town. Brian knew he should be concerned about how long they were gone. There was so much to do, and his absence was unexplained. But the wind in his hair felt great, and Cathy looked wonderful behind the wheel. The moment was not too hard to take.

He let himself go. "So where are we going?" he asked loudly to be heard over the wind.

There was a wide grin on her face as she said, "You'll see."

She turned up the radio and began to sing along with "The Monster Mash." Brian laughed at her imitation of the Boris Karloff accent and then began to sing along.

An hour and a half later, Cathy stopped the car beside cliffs that overlooked a deserted strip of beach. They were consumed by the moment and didn't notice the car that stopped about a hundred yards behind them. The woman who drove the car watched in silence as they got out of the car.

"Come on," Cathy said.

He followed her over to the cliffs. They held hands and looked out across the vast ocean to the horizon with patches of clouds dancing above it.

"It's gorgeous," he said. "I've lived in this city almost forever, and I had no idea there was a place this beautiful within reach."

She nodded. "Let's go down to the beach."

Brian regarded her skeptically. "It's steep, and we're a little overdressed."

"I know." She kicked off her pumps and threw them down on the beach. Then she began to climb down the rocks.

Brian stared after her for a few moments and then grinned and followed her down. When they had climbed down fifteen feet to the beach, they were in an isolated alcove, surrounded by rocky cliffs on three sides while the fourth looked out at endless, blue ocean.

Cathy sat on a rock and peeled off her nylons. "Much better. Now I'm ready for some serious beach walking."

Brian also sat on a rock and took off his shoes and socks, finding it hard to believe that all this was happening on what was supposed to be another day at the office. He watched Cathy staring out at the ocean and was amazed at her beauty. She turned to see him watching her and smiled. She took his hand, and they walked down the beach. Brian felt the wind caressing his face, the warmth of her hand in his, and the sand moving under his feet. Everything else was gone.

When they returned to the alcove, an hour had passed. They stopped to kiss before climbing back up the cliff. The kiss was at first tender and then became passionate. Gulls cried out to the blue, cloudless sky as they soared overhead. The ocean came closer to them with each wave that broke against the rocks encircling the cove.

As Brian looked out across the ocean to see it touching the sky, he couldn't tell where one stopped and the other began. It was all a merging of beautiful blue. It was heaven.

Cathy pulled him close and kissed him softly. "I guess we should go. Sooner or later, we're going to be missed at work."

He nodded reluctantly. They climbed up the rocks, stopping at the top for one last look and one more kiss before walking back to the car.

As they drove back to the city, absorbed in each other, the unidentified car followed at a distance.

Chapter 4

Michael Hayward stood behind his desk with his arms folded, talking into the speakerphone. He spoke to the Chairman of Insignia Insurance about the protections the man might have if International Resource acquired a controlling interest in his company, something they both knew was more than a possibility.

"That's all I can do, Chuck. One year to turn a profit under our plan. You report to me as a division of International Resource. You know the rest." The line was quiet. "If you doubt your willingness or ability to follow my directives, take the package and walk away."

Jackson F. Parker, John to those who knew him well, walked into the office, waving a hand at Michael. He moved toward the couch across the office. In the other hand, he carried a file. The expression on his rotund face was serious, perhaps even sad. He sat so he was looking away from Michael and waited.

"All right, Mike. I understand," Chuck said finally. "I'm going to stay with you and try it. I think we'll get along."

"I think so too, Chuck. Welcome aboard."

After hanging up, Michael smiled at Parker. "Hi, John." He walked over and sat in a chair opposite Parker. The visit was unexpected. It wasn't lost on Michael that most visits with Parker were in Parker's office and were prearranged.

Parker looked at Michael squarely and let out a deep breath. He loosened his coat. "Looks like things are moving along well with Insignia."

"Yes, everything's in place." Michael knew that Insignia had nothing to do with this visit. Parker knew it was a done deal. Michael waited for Parker to speak.

There was a silence while Parker selected his words. "I'm not going to beat around the bush," he finally said. "We've known each other a long time, and I owe it to you to be direct." He looked away for just a moment and then looked directly into Michael's eyes. "Jason Ross is going to take over for me."

Michael was stunned. He felt himself beginning to sweat. "Why, John? What happened? I thought I was the one."

Parker nodded. "I know you did. A lot of people did." He looked at the floor, hesitating. The search for words was uncharacteristic of Parker, who always seemed to know what to say. "You know I think highly of you. You've got one of the keenest senses for business I've ever seen."

"So what is it then? You think Jason Ross is better qualified?"

Parker rubbed a hand across his chin and then leaned toward Michael. "You've done some great things for this company, Michael. But a lot of it's more than making money."

"Like what?"

"Not making mistakes."

"What are we talking about, John?" Michael demanded, his eyes blazing.

Parker lowered his head. "The Westmont Manufacturing deal."

"It closed two months ago. Everything went fine."

"Until now," Parker said.

"Let me in on what's going on," Michael said.

"Your group had control of the project from the ground up."

"That's right."

Parker dropped the file on the coffee table between them. "The company's going to have some problems explaining this, Mike. Westmont has been disposing of hazardous waste improperly for years. There's going to be EPA cleanup liability. It's not clear how bad it's going to be yet, but it will be in the millions. Some say well over two hundred million. Not to mention a lot of negative publicity."

Michael felt a knot in his stomach. He was trying not to appear visibly shaken. "But the contracts contain representations about violation of federal law and hazardous waste." Michael knew that wasn't much of an answer, and he knew that Jackson Parker knew it too.

If we had known this, we would have walked away from the deal. But why didn't we know it? It was the job of my people to be on top of the critical issues, he thought.

"I had Brad Fisher on this. We went over all of it. He said it was all in order, governmental compliance and everything."

Parker reached over and slapped Michael on the shoulder. "I know, but when it all comes out, you know where it's going to land."

Michael just nodded. The pain in his stomach was becoming nausea with the realization that this was his career.

"They're going to look right at you and me, Mike. I'll be all right. I'm retiring anyway. But I won't get away with giving you the top job when this comes out. With the political fallout, the board won't let it happen." He shook his head and then let out a sigh. "There's one other qualified candidate. And now Jason Ross becomes the safer choice."

Michael couldn't think of anything to say. He held his head in his hands silently.

Parker stood and turned to leave. "The announcement won't be made for another three weeks. I wanted you to know as soon as possible." He paused. "I want you to know that I still think you're the best man for the job. I just can't give it to you."

Michael was still nodding, staring at nothing, when Parker left the room and closed the door behind him.

* * *

Michael looked through the file while he waited for Brad Fisher to arrive. It didn't take long to find what he was looking for. The picture was clear. All of it should have been discovered before the deal was closed. He checked the information Parker had left with what was in his own files. He had none of it. But Brad had to have known. Brad had worked on acquisitions for ten years.

There was a knock at the door. "Come in," Michael said, looking up from the file.

The door opened, and Brad Fisher stood in the doorway. His curly blond hair and light mustache made him appear younger than his thirty-five years. His expression said he was some combination of curious and tentative.

"Come in, Brad. Sit down."

"What's up, Chief? Figured it must be important when you pulled me from a meeting with a big lender."

"It is." Michael sat back in his chair and looked into Fisher's eyes. He said nothing. He could see Fisher starting to look uneasy.

"What is it, Michael?" Brad finally asked again.

Michael threw down the file in front of him with critical documents on top. "Explain it."

Brad didn't have to look at the papers on the file long. Michael could see recognition in his expression. He was silent for a few minutes. Michael glared at him and waited.

"Well, sometimes things emerge that you didn't count on when you were checking the deal—-"

Michael interrupted him, "Save it, Brad. You're not talking to anybody you can bullshit. I asked you specific questions about the deal, and you assured me it all checked out. We went over governmental compliances, including waste and environmental.

According to you, the deal was clean. No governmental problems." He pointed to the file. "Some of the approvals were never obtained, and you knew there were environmental cleanup issues." Michael made a fist and shook it in the air. "You knew it, and you sat on it."

Brad was silent, but there was no surprise in his eyes. Michael had lost the top job, what he had he worked for all his life, because of one of his own.

Anger flared in his eyes. "You're through here! Clean out your office and be out of the building within the hour."

Brad looked up at Michael and actually smiled. "I've taken a job reporting to Ross as a vice president," he said calmly.

Michael's eyes glazed over as it all fell into place. The negligence of a subordinate hadn't let him down. It was worse. His enemy had betrayed him. Brad was in Jason Ross' pocket. For a moment, Michael thought he would put a fist into Brad's face. He stared at Brad, who averted his eyes.

"You sold me out, Brad. I'll see that your career is over," Michael said with a deadly edge to his voice.

"I'm sorry, Mike. It was just business. I have greater potential with Ross. I know I'm not moving up any higher than where I am right now if I stay with you. You don't appreciate my talents. So when a chance came to get a promotion under Ross, I had to go for it."

It was the payoff for the ultimate act of disloyalty. Michael had to restrain himself from grabbing Brad by the throat. "I'll see that you don't survive with Ross either, you son of a bitch. Now get out!"

Brad stood and walked to the door without looking back.

* * *

Michael sat with Carol on the patio, sipping a bourbon. She held a glass of white wine and tried to engage him in conversation. It was Saturday at twilight, and Michael had just returned from the office. He was quiet, lost in his thoughts. He had thought about nothing else since his meeting with Parker three days ago. He kept reliving the realization. The betrayal had cost him his ultimate dream. The presidency would never be his. Nothing else seemed to matter.

He looked at Carol, and she smiled at him. Her red hair was clipped up in a bun, revealing her diamond stud earrings. Her soft features were understated. Large green eyes illuminated her small mouth and straight nose. She tried to be supportive, but she would never understand. Michael didn't really expect her to know the depth of his disappointment and anger. No one could.

"You haven't been sleeping much, have you?" she asked with concern.

"No, not much," he replied softly.

"I know how hard this has been, Mike. But at some point, you'll have to accept it and move on."

He was instantly angry. "How can I accept this? I was stabbed in the back. Now that asshole Ross gets the job, and I never move anywhere again."

She walked over and touched his hand gently. "I know, but there's nothing you can do. It's a done deal. Unless Jason Ross drops dead in the next three weeks, he gets the job, and you have to live with it."

Michael was quiet. There were stirrings within him. It took him a few moments to realize that he was reacting to the thoughts of Jason Ross dropping dead. *Maybe it wasn't quite a done deal*, he thought, downing the last of his bourbon.

* * *

Brian pulled into the driveway at seven thirty on Thursday. He walked in the front door and called to see if Barbara were home from the meeting she told him she was going to attend, a fundraiser of some kind.

"Barb," he called from the entryway.

"In here," she yelled. Her voice came from the kitchen.

At the same time, the smells reached Brian's olfactory senses. It was something spicy. He walked into the kitchen to see her pouring beef and sauce over plates of noodles. The adjoining dining room was set for a candlelight dinner.

"Wow," he said.

She grinned. "Your favorite dinner all done and almost on the table. Just like Ozzie and Harriet, don't you think?" She walked over and kissed him on the lips.

"This is great," he said. "Can I help?"

"Sure. Kiss me again."

Brian hesitated and then kissed her. She put her arms around him and kissed back. Putting his arms around her, he realized she wasn't wearing a bra. He kissed her again and then lifted the sweater over her head. She smiled, watching him look at her breasts. She pressed against him and kissed him deeply. Then she pulled off his tie and undid his shirt buttons so nothing was between them.

She looked into his eyes and grinned. "I think dinner's getting cold."

He nodded. "Stroganoff temperature cold. Body temperature hot."

He kissed her again. Then they shed the rest of their clothing and made love on the kitchen floor. It was more spontaneous than they had been in years. The stroganoff was a million miles away.

After the lovemaking, they shared a candlelit dinner, still feeling the glow of intimacy. After dinner, they decided to take a walk. There were few streetlights in the neighborhood. Most of the light came from the stars and the crescent-shaped moon. The night air was calm and cool. They spoke of Brian's new responsibilities and of being rookies in a world of veteran movers and shakers. They spoke of all the political dinners and speeches ahead, and they decided to take a vacation as soon as they could.

They held hands as they walked, stopping to look at a star and to share a kiss.

Somewhere during the walk, Brian remembered just how much he loved Barbara. The eyes and the soul of the woman he had fallen in love with so long ago were still the same. She was still the one.

Brian thought about Cathy. *Was she a new course in my life, or was she a part of finding my way back to Barbara?* For a brief moment, he thought about telling Barbara about Cathy. Then he thought better of it. *What would be gained?* It would be solely to purge his newly discovered conscience. At that moment, Brian decided on his course. He would end it with Cathy, and Barbara need never know.

He looked in Barbara's eyes and said, "I love you so much."

They kissed again, slowly and passionately. That night after they climbed into bed, he kissed her softly on the cheek. "Thank you for a wonderful evening. I had a great time."

She smiled broadly. "Me too. I think I'll be smiling all day tomorrow."

He put his arm around her, and they drifted off to sleep, feeling renewed by their rediscovered passion.

* * *

On Friday evening at seven o'clock, Michael was in his office, waiting for Jason Ross. In the exercise of his upcoming power, Jason would make Michael wait. Just knowing that's what he was doing was humiliating. Michael looked out the window and thought about all he had done to get to the top job. There wasn't much he wouldn't do to get it. That had become clear to him lately ever since Carol's innocent comment about Jason Ross dropping dead.

Michael thought about the betrayal by Brad Fisher, soon to be one of Jason's new vice presidents. He didn't want to give up the fight, but inside he knew it was all over. The decision had been made, and their fates were sealed, irreversibly. Jason Ross would have the top job. Michael would have to work under Jason to survive in the company. Brad Fisher would probably do just fine.

There was a knock at the door, and Jason Ross entered, not waiting for acknowledgment. It was seven fourteen. His close-cropped gray hair and his clean-shaven face gave him the look of a military officer. He carried himself with confidence. His solid six-foot frame was clad in an expensive black suit. It seemed befitting of the occasion. He also wore a smile.

"Hello, Jason," Michael said icily as his competitor planted himself in one of the visitor's chairs across the desk.

"Michael," Jason answered and paused briefly, donning a serious expression. "I guess you're aware of the changes that are coming up."

"You know I am. Congratulations."

Jason nodded an artificial thank you. "I've been doing some serious thinking about the changes that need to happen in the company."

Michael watched him closely, aware that this was the point when he was going to be told that he would be given a small division outside the circle of influence, the corporate equivalent of an exile to Siberia. "What kind of changes?"

"You, for one." Jason's expression was unreadable. "I've thought about it long and hard, and I don't think we can work together. I've decided that, within twenty-four hours after Parker makes his announcement, I want your resignation."

Michael's look was incredulous. "Resign? Why should I?"

"Because I don't trust you," Jason said, leaning forward in his chair. "You've never been behind me on anything, and I don't think that's likely to change."

Michael was taken aback. *Reassignment maybe, but I hadn't expected to be fired.*

"And if I elect not to resign?"

"Don't do it to yourself, Michael. Who's going to want you in their top management if they learn International Resource terminated you?"

Michael sat back in his chair and stared at Jason. He tried to hold on to his composure. Inwardly, he was seething, but he was determined that Jason wouldn't see it. He groped for the right words but could find nothing artful to say.

What came out wasn't planned. "You son of a bitch!"

Jason shook his head. "We've never been on the same team, Michael. We fight each other at every step. We always have. Now that I've got the job you think you should have, I don't see that changing." He stood and walked toward the door. Then he stopped and looked back at Michael. "I'm sorry. I really am." Then he continued out the door.

Michael didn't move. He sat staring at the door. A fury of emotions was beneath the controlled surface he had shown to Jason. He leaned back in his chair and stared at the closed door in disbelief. His whole career, everything he had worked for, was gone. What he had given up all other parts of his life for. It just couldn't be.

He suddenly found himself thinking about his conversation with Carol. He thought again about Jason Ross dropping dead before the announcement of his succession to Parker's throne. Michael realized that, for the first time in his life, he was toying with the idea of killing another human being.

He sat in silence for three hours, never moving from the chair he had occupied during Jason's visit. Finally, at slightly after ten, he picked up his jacket and turned off the office lights. As he walked down the deserted hallways to the elevator, it occurred to Michael that he had forgotten to call Carol, who thought he would be home at eight.

Michael's sudden emergence from the office startled an el-derly man who was vacuuming the carpets in the outer office.

Michael gave him a nod and kept walking and searching for an answer; he had to do something.

He struggled with turbulent emotions, anger that was hard to contain, and fear of a future he couldn't allow. There would be nothing left of his life's work.

As the days passed and the idea became obsession, taking over all of Michael's thoughts, he came to accept it as necessary. It was a business decision. Sometimes the costs in business were high. Sometimes there was just no other choice. Michael knew he was strong enough to do what had to be done. He always had been. He knew that Jason Ross had left him no choice. The decision had been there the entire time, just waiting for him to arrive at the inevitable.

For three days, he thought about the details, coming up with ideas that became plans, strategies he ultimately discarded because they weren't quite right. On Wednesday, Michael had Sheila hold his calls and reschedule appointments. He stayed alone in his office all day. It was almost four o'clock when it finally came to him.

Suddenly he knew exactly what to do, and it had been right in front of him all along. The seeds of the plan had already been sown. Michael felt renewed. He was still in the game. Michael smiled widely as he reached for the phone.

Chapter 5

Brian went the entire week without seeing Cathy. It was more a matter of circumstance than choice, but it helped postpone the inevitable meeting when he would end their relationship. On Sunday night, she had traveled to New York for meetings. On Thursday afternoon, Brian was in the conference room of his offices, meeting with two staffers of Victor Barber, the senior member of the House Budget Committee. The meeting was acknowledgment of his arrival on the scene and to solicit Brian's support for Barber's policies and programs. Senior politicians were always working on one more vote, even when they were on vacation in France, as Barber was now.

Brian excused himself and left the meeting to check on the status of a couple of other projects and because he had consumed too much coffee. He had to urinate so badly he felt that his eyes were turning yellow. It was either take a break or install a catheter. As he left the conference room, a strikingly young volunteer waving in his direction met him.

"Sorry to bother you, Congressman, but there's a Cathy Jenkins from International Resource on the phone. I thought it might be important."

He nodded. "Thanks. I'll take the call."

As he walked away, the assistant called after him, "Line three."

Brian moved to his office and closed the door. He sat down at his desk, picked up the phone, and punched at the third button, which blinked impatiently. He realized he was excited at the prospect of talking to her again.

"Cathy?"

"Hi, Congressman. Remember me?" Her voice was cheery and very warm.

"How could I forget? Our time together is hardly mundane, you know."

She laughed. "I'll say. I think often of our time together."

"I do too." He grinned. "So how's New York?"

"It's the same. The meetings are too long, the people are too serious, and the cabbies are too aggressive."

Brian laughed.

"I hope I didn't interrupt anything too important. I was just thinking about you and ..." Her voice trailed off.

"Yeah, me too. It's good to hear your voice."

"I'll be back tomorrow," she said quickly.

"I remember."

"Can I see you tomorrow night?"

Brian felt his stomach churning. This was not a meeting he looked forward to, but he knew he just couldn't put it off any more. "Sure. What time?"

"Come over about seven thirty, okay?"

"I'll be there."

"Take good care until I see you tomorrow."

"You too. Fly carefully."

"Bye."

"Good-bye." Brian put down the phone with a feeling of discomfort. She was something special. He got the same feelings of excitement every time they spoke. Tomorrow would be hard.

The young assistant knocked on his door. "Congressman, Mr. Dominguez from the governor's office on line one,

Mrs. White of Project Hope is on line four, and your wife is on five. Who should I take messages from?"

"All of them. I have to get back into that meeting. And I have to pee before I explode."

The young woman burst out laughing.

"But you can just tell them I'm in a meeting," Brian said as he ran out of the office.

* * *

Cathy finished her meetings early on Thursday and decided to take a walk down Fifth Avenue to explore the stores. She found herself grinning widely and thinking about Brian as she walked. She thought about his voice on the telephone and his touch on her cheek. She thought about tomorrow night. She couldn't remember ever feeling like this before. She had been in love, but it was never like this, so warm and so fulfilling.

Her step was almost a skip, and the breeze along the avenue felt like it just might lift her off the ground. The thought was corny, but she couldn't help it. She reminded herself of Marlo Thomas doing her "That Girl, I'm in love with the world" walk. She laughed aloud at the thought.

When she got back to the hotel, Cathy called her mother. She was feeling alight with her feelings for Brian, and she felt the urge to share it.

"Hi, Mom," she said cheerily.

"Hi, sweetheart. How's New York?"

"Not as cold or lonely as I might have guessed."

"Your meetings are going good?"

"Yeah, they're fine." Cathy paused. She and her mother had always been able to talk about almost anything, so it was easy to confide in her. "I think I've fallen in love," she blurted out.

"Really? That's wonderful, dear."

Cathy knew her mother meant it. Her mother also knew it had been a long time since she was in love like this. Maybe she never had been.

"Who is he?" her mother asked.

Cathy was careful. Brian was still married, and she would get into that slowly. "He's someone I met through the campaign work I've been doing. His name is Brian."

Then came that uniquely parental welcome, "Will you bring him to dinner?"

"Yes, I will. At the first opportunity."

Her mother seemed to be catching some of the excitement. "Is it already serious?"

"Yes, I think it is." She paused. "I don't know when I've been this happy."

"I can hardly wait to meet him. Bring him home soon."

"I will," Cathy replied, hoping that she would. She sensed that Brian loved her too and wanted to be with her. They would work it out. "I just wanted you to be the first to know. Give my love to Dad for me."

"All right. I will. I love you. Good-bye, baby."

As she hung up the telephone, Cathy felt light-headed. She thought about her conversation with Brian. She liked replaying the part when they said they missed one another. It seemed as if he was as happy to speak with her as she had been to talk to him. She thought about seeing him tomorrow night, and she thought about their future, the future they would make together.

* * *

On Friday morning, Barbara kissed Brian good-bye at the door. She was warm and affectionate, a carryover of the closeness from their evening of rediscovery. It should have been great, but with thoughts of seeing Cathy crossing his mind, Brian felt uneasy. He touched Barbara's cheek and told her he would be late. They made plans to have breakfast and spend time together in the morning.

The day passed slowly, and Brian had a hard time keeping his thoughts on the business that needed his attention. His mind would stray to his memorable days and nights with Cathy and then to his life with Barbara. He thought of the renewal in his relationship with Barbara and realized how much she meant to him. He also thought of the arousal and the warmth he shared with Cathy. By the end of the day, Brian had played and replayed countless scenes with each woman. He felt no more enlightened and just as nervous about the evening with Cathy. He had accomplished almost nothing at the office, and he had a headache.

Brian arrived at Cathy's apartment at eight o'clock. She opened the door and smiled. She wore a soft blue, low-neck dress, and a string of pearls. Her light makeup added a glow to her face.

"I've missed you," she said and threw her arms around him.

The scent of her perfume was intoxicating, like ubiquitous wildflowers in a spring meadow. She looked into his eyes, and Brian heard himself telling her that he had missed her, too. And he had. She brought her lips to his and kissed him passionately. He found himself immediately aroused.

"Come with me," she said and led him to a formal dinner for two laid out in the dining room.

The china and silverware were in place, the wine glasses were full, and the fire blazed, casting shadows across the wall behind the table. The lighting from the overhead chandelier was soft and diffuse. The effect was warmth and isolation.

"I can't believe you've done all this when you've been in New York all week. It's incredible," Brian said appreciatively.

"I've had lots of time to plan it." She kissed him again. "I can't tell you how good it is to see you."

Brian had not envisioned it happening this way. This was supposed to be the sobering discussion of why they couldn't possibly go on together. He thought of all that Cathy had done in preparation. She was so happy. It just was not the right moment. He told himself that he would wait as he kissed her deeply and then gazed into those eyes that seemed to reach out to him. He gave himself to the moment, and they spoke of his week and her travels. She served a wonderful shrimp scampi, and each drank three glasses of wine.

They cleared the table and then moved to the couch in the living room. As they sat in front of the fireplace with the last of the wine, Brian could feel it going to his head. Cathy toasted to them. He toasted to her smile. She leaned toward him and then looked up and kissed him. They were soon locked in an embrace with the passion growing. They left the couch without letting each other go and made their way to the bedroom. They made love in her bed and then fell asleep in each other's arms.

It was one o'clock when Brian awoke. He looked around to get his bearings. He saw the red digital readout of the alarm clock and began to dress quickly. He was going to be late again. He briefly wondered why Barbara had never asked about his late arrivals before. He was grateful for her trust, the trust he was betraying again.

Cathy sat up in bed, letting the covers fall to her waist. Brian admired her full breasts, and she smiled when she saw him looking.

"Can't you stay with me tonight?" she asked. "I'd really like to make you breakfast in the morning. Maybe even make love again after breakfast."

Brian smiled at the thought. "I'd like that too, but I can't stay. I have to get home."

She watched him finish dressing and then motioned him over to the bed. She gave him a long, passionate kiss and told him that she loved him. He smiled, but remained silent. He didn't know what to say.

"Tomorrow night around seven?" she asked.

"I'll have to call you tomorrow." Brian kissed her again and then walked toward the door.

"I was thinking we could go away for a weekend in a couple of weeks," Cathy called to him.

He nodded at her. "I'm not sure when I can get a whole weekend right now. We'll talk more tomorrow."

He left the apartment, cursing himself for not having straightened things out and for sleeping with her again. And there was something else; a part of him just didn't want to let her go.

It was after one-thirty when he climbed into bed with Barbara. She put her arms around him and kissed him gently on the lips.

"I missed you, Brian," Barbara whispered softly. "I love you." She softly touched his cheek.

"I love you, too, Barb." He drew her to him and kissed her forehead, the bridge of her nose, and then her lips. He gave her a reassuring smile. "Good night, sweetheart," he said and then turned over.

Soon he heard the soft and rhythmic sounds of her breathing as she slept. Brian lay awake until after four o'clock, consumed by conflicting feelings and the long overdue guilt he had been expecting.

Chapter 6

Cathy met Brian standing on the beach, waiting for her. She ran across the sand to him. He opened his arms and wrapped them around her, picking her up and spinning her in the air. He whispered, "I love you" and then kissed her softly on the mouth. They put their arms around one another and began to walk along the deserted beach as the sun began to disappear beyond the horizon, followed by a magnificent trail of red and orange. Cathy looked up at the love on his face, drinking it all in as one of life's perfect moments. The ocean touched their feet, and its sounds were the musical soundtrack to a love that was forever.

For that infinite moment, Cathy's world was all it could ever be. Happiness and love moved over her and filled her with the deepest contentment she had ever known. Then it all began to change. The ocean was gone. Now she and Brian were walking faster through a jungle. What had been sand was now trees, vines, and thick vegetation. They were trying to get away from something. There was a pounding in the background, like a native drum. She looked at Brian, and his expression had changed to concern. He held onto her hand, and they began to run. The pounding grew louder. Something was getting closer.

Brian's face had changed again. The concern had become fear. He clutched Cathy's hand tightly, and they ran faster. The pounding was deafening and seemed to be directly behind them. Cathy looked over her shoulder. There was nothing.

Then through a fog, Cathy began to realize that the jungle was a dream. She slowly awoke, realizing she was alone in bed. She was relieved that the fear was just part of a dream and then suddenly sad that the depth of love and devotion in Brian's eyes had been part of that dream.

She looked over at the red digits of her clock radio. It was twelve after two. Brian had been gone just over an hour. She heard a knock at her door and recognized it as the pounding that had made its way into her dream. She slowly walked to the closet and put on her robe. She walked to the front door and peered out through the peephole. Then she unlocked the deadbolt and opened the door.

Chapter 7

Barbara climbed out of bed and made her way to the bathroom, striking the doorjamb with her shoulder in her grogginess. She strained to see the digital readout on the bedside alarm. *Seven o'clock*, she thought.

Brian was just beginning to come to. Through a veil of fog, he heard someone say "Dammit." Then he heard the shower. He fell back to sleep, and the sounds became a waterfall in a lush forest. When he next awoke, Barbara was putting on makeup by the dresser. Brian made his way over to kiss her.

"Morning, darling," she said with a warm smile. "Coffee's on."

"Sounds great. Just a quick shower and I'll be ready." He kissed her again and then made his way toward the bathroom.

It was just before eight o'clock when they sat on patio chairs with hot coffee to take in the cool spring air. It was one of those mornings Brian loved. The sky was amazing, occasional swirling clouds so far apart as to look lonely against the uninterrupted light blue behind them. The air seemed extraordinarily breathable with a light breeze moving through the backyard. Birds chirped and sang competing melodies from every direction. Both Brian and Barbara were dressed in jeans and a sweater to take the edge off the morning briskness.

"This is wonderful," he said, glancing around at the view. "I feel like I'm a million miles away from everything."

She nodded and then looked at him thoughtfully. "It feels like it used to when we first started out, when we used to take every spare moment we could find to get away together. Remember?"

"Yeah, I remember," he said wistfully. "Good memories."

"And we went for walks and to some cozy, out-of-the-way place for breakfast. And there was nothing else but you and me."

"I remember." He was quiet for a moment. Then he looked into her eyes. They were somehow alight. "Let's do it again. Now. Today. We'll take a walk and then go to Rosie's for breakfast. Just us for the whole weekend."

She smiled happily and touched his hand. "That's a wonderful idea. I can be ready in fifteen minutes."

As they stood up to get ready, the telephone rang.

"I'll get it," Brian said and ran into the den.

"Hello?"

"Brian?"

He recognized Dan Anderson's voice. Dan was almost a caricature, short, chubby, and bald and never seen without a large unlit cigar hanging from his lips. They had been friends for years. Dan was a freelance journalist, and they had met in the early years of Brian's law practice. One of several controversial cases Brian had handled had caused the reporters to swarm. Dan had been the only one not to quote him out of context. From then on, Dan had been the first to get anything Brian had for the media. Even now, when Brian was much more frequently quoted in light of his newfound status, he still went first to Dan. Dan treated him right. Dan had even done some volunteer work for Brian's campaign.

"Hi, Dan. What's up?"

"You watching TV?" Dan asked, sounding out of breath.

"No. We're sitting out back, enjoying nature and caffeine."

"Turn it on quick. Channel four."

"Why?"

"Just do it!" Dan nearly shouted.

Brian grabbed the remote and pushed the power button. There was an electrical wake-up surge, and the picture took shape. He hit another button and had channel four.

"At this hour, not much else is known," was the first thing he caught.

A woman dressed for the Arctic was standing on a sidewalk and speaking into a microphone covered by a big number four.

"Her name was Cathy Jenkins. We know she worked for International Resource Corporation in marketing. We know that, sometime late last night or early this morning, she was brutally murdered, apparently by someone she let into her home. We'll keep you posted as this tragic story unfolds. This is Linda Morales, Channel Four News."

Brian stared at the television. "Oh my God," he whispered.

"Brian?" he heard as if the voice were far away.

Brian reeled with shock and disbelief. It was all he could do to speak. "Yeah, I'm here," he said, nearly choking on the words.

"She was a good lady. I hope they get the son of a bitch who did this," Dan said.

There was silence while Brian tried to collect his thoughts and his composure. "You knew her?"

"Yeah. I met her a couple times at your campaign headquarters. Likable woman."

Brian was trying to stay in the conversation. "Thanks for calling, Dan. Thanks for letting me know."

Dan said something, but Brian wasn't sure what. He just could not stay with the conversation. Brian hung up the phone before realizing he hadn't actually said good-bye. His chest was suddenly tight, and he was having a hard time getting air. *Who could have done this? No one would want to kill Cathy*, Brian thought hard. *What time was it when I left?* He pushed another button on the remote and found another news segment.

"All we know about this brutal crime is that she was apparently struck in the head several times with a blunt object," another female reporter was saying. "Police say there are no signs of forced entry and the murder weapon has not been recovered or, as yet, identified. Carla Dillon, ABC News."

Emotions swarmed over Brian—grief, fear, and guilt all at once. He suppressed a strong urge to panic. *Cathy couldn't be dead. It just couldn't be.* He had been with her only eight hours ago. She had held him close and told him that she loved him. She had been content, and everything was fine when he left her apartment. He remembered locking the door when he left. The news reports were baffling.

No sign of forced entry. Did she open the door and let someone in? Brian thought about the dinner they had shared. *The wine in front of the fire. Her sitting up in bed to ask me to stay as I was dressing.* He found himself fighting off the urge to cry.

Brian looked up and saw Barbara standing there, watching him expectantly. All of a sudden, it hit him with the force of a freight train. His fingerprints were everywhere in Cathy's apartment. They would have a suspect in no time. Maybe they had already identified him. They would be looking for him with questions. He would have to explain to Barbara and the whole world why he had been in Cathy's apartment.

He opened his mouth to speak to Barbara about the call from Dan, but no words came out. Then the next revelation hit him. They would know that she had intercourse shortly before she died. They would ask Brian about that too. He felt a wave of nausea sweep over him, and for a moment, he felt that he would throw up. He put his head between his legs and waited for it to pass.

"What's the matter?" Barbara asked with concern. "What can I get you?"

"I'll be all right," Brian whispered, raising his hand weakly. "I just felt sick for a moment." He suddenly remembered there were condoms in her nightstand with his fingerprints on the box.

Barbara walked over and put her arm around him. He knew she had seen part of the last news segment and his expression as he watched. *Did she perceive the extent of the loss to me? Was she wondering about my overreaction?*

"I'll get you some water," she said, turning toward the kitchen.

Brian sat staring into the backyard, seeing nothing but Cathy's face and then the vivid image of the news clip, a blood-stained carpet in front of the couch where they had sat together last night, and where they had made love in front of the fire.

His mind kept moving between the tragedy and the trail, the indelible path that clearly led to his doorstep. *When and where had we been seen together? Neighbors would have seen me coming and going. Maybe they wouldn't remember me.*

His thoughts returned to the inescapable, his fingerprints. The police would soon find him and watch his expression while he tried to explain. They would learn that he had been there regularly and he was there shortly before the murder. They would conclude that he might have been there at the time of the murder. And they would learn about the affair. He would soon be the primary suspect in the death of his lover. There were lots of obvious motives, such as keeping his wife and maybe his constituents from finding out about the affair. He would have no credibility in proclaiming his innocence. It felt like the walls were closing in around him.

Barbara was saying something to him. She was asking whether he was okay. *How many times had she asked?* Brian wondered. He was fighting the panic that seemed like it might overtake him at any moment. She had put down the glass of water some time before.

"Yes, I'm starting to feel a little better." He reached for the water and drank deeply.

Barbara held his hand and smiled at him compassionately. "She worked with you at the campaign office?"

He nodded. He didn't expect the emotion that came out when he spoke. "How could this happen? Who would kill her?"

"Did you know her well?"

It was hard to know what to say. "She was a nice person. She seemed to care about what she did."

Brian thought about how that sounded. *What bullshit.* He knew instinctively that there was really no choice. He had to tell Barbara, and it had to be now. Then he had to go to the police before they came to him. He had to tell them he had been to Cathy's apartment before they told him he had been there and then read him his rights. He had to tell Barbara first. He glanced over at the clock, as if it would tell him how long it would be before the police arrived. It was ten forty.

The television flashed images of the outside of Cathy's apartment. A barricade of yellow police tape was winding its way around trees in the narrow front yard, a flimsy plastic line that the crowd of onlookers respected as they spoke in inaudible tones and pointed to the building. The camera panned the faces and then returned to the building, focusing on two uniformed officers who stood at the door. One stood with his arms crossed, staring at the crowd as if they might be readying to stampede him. The other shielded a match from the wind and lit a cigarette, looking visibly bored, biding his time.

Brian tried to find the words. He looked down at the floor and then back to Barbara.

"What is it, Brian?" she asked, frowning.

"Barbara, there's something I have to tell you."

She nodded encouragingly. The look was warm and understanding.

"I want you to know …"

The telephone rang, and Brian jumped. He looked at it like it was about to explode. On the third ring, he picked it up.

"Hello?"

"Is this Brian Madsen?" It was a male voice he didn't recognize.

"Yes," Brian said in a cracking voice.

"You've seen the news, haven't you?"

"Who is this?"

He ignored the question. "Get rid of your wife if she's there. We need to talk."

"Who is this, and what do you want?" Brian knew he was getting louder. "I don't need this."

The voice became slower and more deliberate. "Don't hang up." There was a brief pause and then, "You want information, or do you want to be arrested? Is your wife right there?"

"Yes," Brian said more calmly.

"Find a way to send her out of the room."

Brian put his hand over the mouthpiece and looked at Barbara. He saw a worried look on her face.

"Who is it?" she asked.

"I don't know yet." Brian made himself breathe deeply, trying to relax. He finished off the water and handed her the glass. "Would you mind getting me some more?" It was hopelessly lame, but whatever worked. She looked at him for a moment with her eyes questioning. Then she left the room.

Brian put the receiver to his ear.

"Have you told anyone yet?" he spoke in riddles.

"Told anyone what?"

"Don't waste time. You and I both know your fingerprints are all over her place. You were there just last night until after one o'clock."

Brian felt like he had been punched in the stomach. He was suddenly ill, feeling like he might vomit. He drew in a deep breath. Then it occurred to him. He was talking to the killer. *How else would this guy know all these details?*

Brian was searching for words. "What do you want? Did you kill her?"

"What I want is cooperation. I get it. Then you don't face murder charges and spend the rest of your life in prison ... or worse. I want you to know that everything has been dusted. No fingerprints have been left in the apartment. All evidence of your presence has been removed."

"Why?"

"I told you. I want your cooperation. If I get it, you're not implicated in any way. If I don't, you're in jail." There was silence. Then he said, "The other thing you should know is that I have a number of things that came from Ms. Jenkins' home that still contain your fingerprints. One of them might just be the murder weapon. I'd say that leaves you rather vulnerable, wouldn't you?"

Brian nodded slowly as Barbara returned with his water. "Yes," he said, in a tone he hoped sounded calm.

"There's no reason for any of these items to find their way to the police. If you cooperate, no one will ever see them."

Brian lost control and screamed out, "You son of a bitch. Why the fuck did you do it?"

"If you don't cooperate, you'll have the opportunity to explain your fingerprints on the murder weapon. Think you can do that?"

Brian clenched his fist but remained silent.

"And let's not forget, you were the last one to see her alive, very soon before she died."

Brian ran a hand through his hair. It all had to be some kind of a nightmare. He looked into Barbara's eyes and saw the fear he felt. Then he returned to the voice on the phone. "What do you want?"

"All in good time. Right now, I want you to know that there is no trail that leads to you yet, but that can change in a hurry. I'll call you back at two o'clock this afternoon. Until then, don't talk to the police. If you invite them in, you'll never hear from me again, and the evidence we spoke of will find its way to the authorities." There was a brief pause. "One more thing. Don't tell your wife anything."

There was the ring of a dial tone in Brian's ear. Brian slowly put the phone back in its cradle and looked at Barbara.

"What did he say?" she asked.

"He said he'll call back at two o'clock and not to call the police."

"Did he kill her?"

"I don't know." Brian remembered the admonition not to tell her anything. He selected his words carefully. "I think so. And I think he might be working on trying to blame me."

Barbara's eyes widened. "How can he do that? You barely knew her."

"I know, but he was very threatening. I'm not sure what he'll do."

"Someone you knew was murdered last night, and we may have just spoken to the killer. We've got to call the police," she said as she began pacing in front of him.

Brian was silent. To bring the police to the caller would be to guarantee he became a suspect. He thought about what the man had said about his prints on the murder weapon. He had to convince Barbara that it was best to wait.

He shook his head. "And tell them what? That we may have just talked to an anonymous killer? If we do, we'll never identify this guy."

She stopped pacing and looked at him quizzically. "Why is he calling back at two o'clock?"

"I don't know. He says he wants me to cooperate with him on something, whatever that means."

"Why would you cooperate with him on anything? He's a killer," she said incredulously.

Brian could feel perspiration beading on his forehead. He didn't know what to tell her. "Let's just wait for two o'clock. He'll call back, and we'll learn more."

"Why don't we call the police? They can have the line tapped by the time he calls back."

Brian's throat was dry. He grabbed for the glass of water. All he needed was a police bug on the line while the caller talked about his fingerprints being all over everything. It occurred to Brian that everything had changed. Before the call, he had made up his mind to tell Barbara and then go to the police. Now he wasn't going to do either. If he cooperated with this guy, he would never be a suspect. Barbara would never have to find out.

Brian looked up at Barbara, and he knew what to say. "If we get in the police to tap the phone, he'll know. He won't call back. Let's just wait for two o'clock and find out more." When she was slow to respond, he added, "There's no real downside to waiting. We can always call the police after he calls back."

She hesitated and then reluctantly nodded concession to the plan. Brian hugged her and told her, "Everything will be all right." Even as he said it, he somehow knew better.

They refilled their coffee cups and then returned to the patio. Brian stared at the springtime beauty of the green hills behind the house, seeing none of it. He was visualizing the impending disaster when his involvement with Cathy came out. When it became clear that he slept with her last night, the last night of her life. When the evidence was delivered to the police, with his fingerprints on whatever the murder weapon happened to be, his marriage and his career would be over; he would go to prison for life, or he would die. The caller controlled all that would happen to Brian.

Brian could not allow himself to think about Cathy being dead. *Survival first and then grief.* He looked over at Barbara. She was staring straight ahead, consumed by thoughts of her own, undoubtedly wondering whether she should have gone along with not calling the police. There was so much that Brian knew he should tell her, so much that kept them at a distance. He knew he wouldn't tell her, at least not yet. At least not until after two o'clock.

Words exchanged were few. At one forty-five, they sat in the den watching the phone and waiting.

Barbara took Brian's hand and held it tightly. "Are you sure we're doing the right thing?" Her voice had a helpless quality to it.

"No, I'm not sure. I just don't know what else to do." He stood up and put his arms around her. He couldn't remember the last time he had attempted to comfort her like this. "It'll be okay." His words were soft and he hoped reassuring, even though he felt there was little to feel comforted about.

At one fifty-eight, the phone rang. Brian picked it up before the second ring. "Hello?" Barbara saw the look of frustration on his face. "I'll have her call you back later, Mom. She's in the shower." Brian was silent as Barbara's mother spoke. "Okay, I'll tell her. She'll call you as soon as possible." His face gave away his impatience. "Yeah, sounds good. We'll talk about it a little later when she calls you back. Bye, Mom."

He put down the phone and checked his watch. It was two o'clock. The minutes passed slowly, and the phone didn't ring. Brian stared at it, hoping the caller hadn't changed his mind. *Maybe he had called and got the busy signal. Perhaps he wouldn't try again.* Brian needed to talk to him again, to figure out a way to stop all this before it came crashing down around him. It was ten after two when the phone rang again.

"Hello?" Brian said quickly.

"Brian Madsen." It was not a question. The voice was the same.

"Yes, this is Brian Madsen."

"I'm pleased there are no police."

Brian instinctively looked out the living room window to the street as if he might see the man standing there, looking in at him. It was clear that someone was watching him.

"What do you want?" he demanded.

"I want the same as you, Brian. I want things done quietly and quickly."

"What things?"

There was a long silence, which worked effectively for emphasis. Brian was listening carefully. "I want you to kill a man."

This time silence accompanied Brian's shock. Then he became angry. "I'm not going to kill anyone."

"I suggest you take your time and think about it. I'll give you a couple of hours, and you want to be extremely careful because you are betting your whole life on this decision."

"You son of a bitch! I'm not going to be blackmailed by some fucking criminal." Brian looked up at Barbara. Her face was full of questions. He wiped the sweat from his forehead and took a deep breath.

"When you reflect on it, you'll see that you really don't have a choice." The voice was calm, which only served to make Brian feel more helpless and angrier.

"I do have a choice. I can go to the police with this and let them find you."

"You could go to the police, that's true. But that wouldn't be too smart. All roads lead to you, Brian. Remember? It won't matter much if you go to them or they come to you. The result is the same if they have the murder weapon with your fingerprints on it, wouldn't you agree?"

There was silence. Then the caller said, "Just don't make the mistake of underestimating me. If you think about what happened to Ms. Jenkins, you'll know there's not much I won't do to get what I need. Oh, and one more thing; I'll know if you talk to the police. If you do, the evidence gets delivered, and you never hear from me again. I'll call you back at five o'clock. I'll expect your decision then."

The line went dead. Brian held the phone at arm's length and stared at it as if it might yield a clue to the man's whereabouts.

Then it occurred to him that it just might. He pushed the asterisk and then numbers six and nine on his telephone. There was ringing on the other end. Brian let it ring ten times and then hung up. He thought about how easy it would be to trace the call if he called the police. *Then what? Like the man said, all the evidence would point to me. The killer would see to that. Or the man could save me, leaving my tracks covered.*

Brian felt a strange sensation of gratitude to the lunatic for having sanitized the apartment. The thankfulness yielded to anger at himself for making his self-preservation a priority over catching this guy, finding the truth, and owning up to his involvement with Cathy.

Barbara touched his hand, bringing him out of his thoughts. "What now?"

Brian shook his head. "I don't know. He wants me to kill a man. Maybe I'll tell him I'll do it. Then we'll have more to go to the police with."

"We have to tell them now, Brian. We can't play games with this guy. What happens when he finds out you're not really going to do it?"

"By then we have more information for the police, so they can get this guy." He touched her cheek. "It's only three more hours."

Brian realized he was shaking. Maybe it was because he was trying to convince Barbara to do something he didn't want to do. He never wanted to hear the voice on the phone again. Perhaps it was the total lack of control over what was happening to him.

Barbara looked unconvinced. "We can make it three more hours," she said as if to reassure herself. She rubbed her hands together nervously and then nodded.

The clock moved slowly. At two forty, the phone rang, and Barbara had a short conversation with her mother. Brian could see that Barbara's mind wasn't on the conversation. She had all the right words but was just going through the motions.

At four o'clock, the phone rang again. Brian stared at it until the third ring with his heart pounding. When he answered, a computerized voice asking survey questions about coffee consumption greeted him. The immediate sense of relief, of buying time, quickly yielded to frustration. Brian wondered if he would make it for another hour.

* * *

The unmarked Dodge rolled out of the police parking lot at Parker Center and moved toward the freeway. "So what do you think we get out of this guy?" asked the young uniformed officer who sat in the passenger seat. He spoke to an older man with the close-cropped hair who wore a baggy blue suit and drove like he was late for something important.

The older man shrugged. "I don't know. Probably nothing. But the only way to get to the bottom line of the investigation is to talk to everyone who hung out with or even heard of the victim."

"Is this just the training speech, or are you about to give me something worthwhile here?" the young man tossed out, grinning.

"Did they send me a cop or a fucking comedian? There's already too damned many uniformed comedians on the street."

"Levity is hard to come by on the street. I'm just here to lighten the load."

The older man rolled his eyes.

"But what do you think the new congressman knows about this dead woman? What's her name? Jenkins. Where's the connection?" the younger officer asked.

"The only connection is that she did some volunteer work to help get him elected."

"That's it?"

"Yeah, so far. He probably doesn't even know this broad."

The young man furrowed his brow. "What did they get from the scene?"

"Not a fucking thing. Cleaner than a baby's newly powdered ass."

"No shit? There's always something, right?"

"Usually. This time it was clean. I think too clean."

The rookie's face had a perplexed look as he asked, "What does that mean?"

"It means this whole thing was likely premeditated, which means it wasn't likely any sort of a heat-of-passion killing. It doesn't look like her boyfriend caught her fucking somebody else."

"You have a way with words, you know?" The younger man grinned. "So what are we talking about? A drug hit or something?"

"I'd be surprised. This broad doesn't fit the profile for that kind of a hit. Nothing around her looks like drug dealing."

"Did you say fit the profile? As in psychological profile? Pretty high tech, college-type shit for a career street cop, isn't it?"

"Fuck you, junior. Shut up, and you'll learn something."

The young man held up his hands in a halting gesture. "Okay, I yield to your wisdom, oh master. In the meantime, let's eat before we go see this guy. It's after three thirty, and I haven't eaten anything yet today. Besides, I don't think I can talk to a politician on an empty stomach."

The older man nodded agreement and then turned the car toward Rosie's diner. "You're right. Politicians are even harder to put up with than you are."

Brian stood alone in the front yard. He scanned the large, two-story homes of his neighbors, looking for any clue, wondering if one of them concealed a caller who would be in a position to see if the police arrived. There was nothing remotely conspicuous or unusual in the appearance of any of the houses. No one looked like he or she didn't fit. There were just normal neighborhood sounds: a couple of children going by on bicycles, the distant sound of a barking dog, and a cacophony of bird songs coming from the overhead trees.

Brian thought about Cathy. He thought about her smile and the way she had touched his hand when they were alone. He thought about the look of love on her face when she had asked him if they could go away for the weekend just last night.

Then the images changed to the photographs run and rerun by television news—vivid stains on the carpet, a gurney, and a body—her body—covered by a black sheet being taken from the apartment. In the face of the tragedy, he was denying her, trying to keep her at a distance so he wouldn't be implicated. Brian began to sob aloud. He hoped Barbara wouldn't hear him, but he couldn't stop crying.

At four-thirty, the doorbell rang. Barbara opened the door to see a man of about fifty in an ill-fitting blue suit and a uniformed police officer, whom she guessed was in his late twenties. The uniformed officer stood with his hands on his hips and waited.

The blue-suited man ran a hand through his short, gray hair before saying, "Mrs. Madsen?"

Barbara eyed him cautiously. "Yes. How can I help you?"

"Your husband home, ma'am?" He sounded politely impatient.

Barbara nodded.

"I'm Sergeant Merrick. This is Officer Palmer. May we take a few minutes of his time?"

Barbara almost asked what this was about and then thought better of it. "Sure, I'll get him. Please step inside."

Both took stepped inside, and the uniformed officer removed his hat. Barbara turned and walked toward the living room, finding Brian there as she entered the room. She let out an embarrassing yelp at the surprise, and then heard one of the officers chuckle behind her. She turned to see the older man giving the uniformed officer a dirty look.

"Brian, these officers want to talk to you."

He nodded and walked toward the front door. She followed him back to where the men waited.

As Brian approached the two men, he reached out a hand, first to the older man. "Gentlemen, I'm Brian Madsen. How can I help you?" He sounded serious and confident, but his heart was racing. He felt the way he thought a guilty suspect might feel when he was scared that he might give something away.

"Mr. Madsen, I'm Sergeant Merrick. This is Officer Palmer." They nodded acknowledgment to one another.

Then Merrick continued, "I don't know if you've heard yet, but someone you know has been killed." He waited for reaction.

Probably watching for a lie, Brian thought.

Brian nodded slightly after a moment. "We've seen it on TV. It's horrible."

"You know her well, sir?"

He asked the big question right away. Brian knew there was no time to pause and think it over. "No, not well. She worked as a volunteer for my campaign office."

Merrick nodded. "She work closely with you?"

Brian shook his head. "No, she worked with volunteer campaign supervisors."

"What kinds of things did she do for the campaign?"

"Just basic volunteer stuff. Grassroots campaigning. Calling up potential voters to encourage them to vote and stuffing envelopes. That kind of thing."

Merrick was nodding again. "So you didn't see much of her?"

Brian felt himself beginning to sweat. "No, not much."

"Just occasionally in the office?"

"Yeah, that's right," Brian said without hesitation.

Merrick rubbed his chin, pausing. "You ever see her outside the office?"

Jesus Christ, Brian thought, *does this guy know something?*

Barbara spoke up. "I think I remember seeing her at the inaugural for Brian. That's the only time though."

"Any other times you've seen her outside of business?" Merrick asked without turning away from Brian.

"None that I can think of." Brian crossed his arms in a nervous gesture.

Merrick shot a glance at Palmer, who remained expressionless. Then Merrick looked back at Brian. "She ever talk to you about her personal life? Anyone she was involved with? Maybe someone harassing her or a person she wanted to get away from?"

"No, I don't recall anything like that," Brian said lamely.

"You know who she was involved with? I mean, anyone she knew intimately?"

Brian answered quickly, "No, I don't know."

Merrick furrowed his brow. "We think she knew the guy who did this."

As Merrick studied him, Brian felt like his legs might give out.

"She let the guy in."

Brian shook his head in disbelief. Merrick stayed fixed on Brian for a moment and then turned to go, signaling the ever-silent Palmer with a slap on the arm. "Call me if you think of anything that might help." He handed Brian a card and gestured a farewell to Barbara, and the two men left. It was seven minutes to five.

Chapter 8

Brian and Barbara sat at the dining room table looking intermittently at each other and then at the telephone. Barbara touched his hand and gave him a strained smile. At precisely five o'clock, the phone rang. Brian looked at Barbara, noting the nervousness in her expression.

He picked up the phone on the second ring. "Hello?"

"Make your decision?" There was no patience in the voice this time.

"Maybe. If I say I'll do it, how do I know what you'll do?"

"You don't. You just know what happens if you don't." The man paused. "It's much better if we both get what we want, isn't it?"

Brian didn't know what to do. He had to buy some time. "All right. Who?"

"Jason Ross."

"Why do you want him killed?" Brian asked nervously.

"That's not information you need."

Brian felt a sense of doom, waves breaking over his head that would soon engulf him.

"You will do it on Tuesday night in the parking garage at 600 Fifth Street. He leaves his office between eight and ten. You'll be waiting near his car, fire two shots to the head, and then you're gone. You take the cash and credit cards from his wallet and leave the empty wallet with the body. Then you drive up to Ninth Street, turn right, and drive for about a mile. You'll open your window, drop the credit cards out, and finally go home. If anyone ever makes any connection to you, you will say that you and your wife were home watching videos that night."

Brian could feel himself shaking. "Why am I taking credit cards to throw them out the window of my car?"

"In that neighborhood, there's no shortage of street life. Someone will find them quickly. That someone will use them, and that lucky soul will be the suspect in the killing. Robbery will be the motive. None of it will come near you."

"I don't know that I can kill anyone." Brian's voice was cracking.

The voice was soft and firm. "You have no choice. At six thirty tonight, you'll pick up an envelope. It will contain what you need."

"Look, I just don't know that I can do it!"

"Listen carefully, Brian. It's not just your future that depends on this. Think about your family. Keep them safe. I know you'll find the strength."

"You son of a bitch!"

"Don't waste time. You have fifteen minutes to get to the corner of Third and Main. It will take you every bit of that time to get there. One of the phones on the corner will ring, and you'll be told where to go next. Got it?"

"Yes. I have it." Brian held his head with his free hand.

"And be alone, Brian. I'll know."

"Okay," Brian said softly.

"One more thing. If you go to the police or get anyone else involved, I'll know. Don't do it, or the police will have all the evidence I have." There was a brief silence before the man continued, "Have you told your wife about you and Cathy Jenkins?"

He didn't wait for an answer. The line went dead.

Brian put down the phone slowly and looked over at Barbara. "He wants me to kill a guy named Jason Ross. I'm supposed to do it Tuesday night in a parking structure downtown. You're to be my alibi if needed. We're supposed to say we were watching videos together."

"Jesus—-"

"I'm supposed to be at a downtown phone booth in fifteen minutes for more instructions. If I don't go right now, I won't make it," Brian interrupted.

Barbara shook her head. "This is crazy, Brian. Let's go to the police."

"Hold on just a little longer," Brian said weakly. "I'll find out more and then we'll figure out what to do."

"Why do we have to learn more? Just give the whole thing over to the police."

He saw the worry in her eyes and held her hands in his. "Hang in there just a little longer."

She was silent. A tear was in her eye. Then she nodded gently. Her expression said she didn't understand. Brian kissed her and then stood to go.

"At least let me come with you," she said.

"No," he said. "I have to go alone. Besides, I don't know that it's safe."

"Of course it's not safe. None of this is safe."

"I'll be back as quickly as I can." He kissed her again and then walked to the front door.

Brian drove at top speeding, and then left his car in a spot left 'no-parking,' a couple of blocks from First and Main as he had no more time. He ran two long blocks toward the telephones at the corner of Main and Third. It was starting to drizzle. He glanced at his watch. He had two minutes. The run took three. He arrived at the bank of silent phones in time for the cloudburst. Within a moment, he was soaked as he stood watching and hoping that he hadn't missed the call, hoping it wasn't all over, and wanting something to happen that kept the evidence of his involvement with Cathy from the police.

Two more minutes passed. Brian paced anxiously. When the phone rang, he jumped, startled by the expected. He picked up the phone on the far right on its first ring. He said nothing.

"Hello, Brian," the now-familiar voice said.

"What now?"

"There's an alley off Temple, south of Los Angeles Street. Go into the alley about thirty feet, and you'll see two trash cans on the left. Look underneath the second can. I'll call you at home."

"When?"

"Tonight. And I'll know if you talked to anyone." The line went dead.

"Shit," Brian mumbled as he slammed down the phone.

He turned and walked toward his car, thinking about Cathy. The rain came down harder, and he was soaked. He didn't care. He wondered if she had let the killer into her apartment. He wondered how much he would miss her when all of this stopped long enough to let him feel her loss.

Brian pulled a parking ticket from his windshield and stuffed it in the glove box. Then he drove toward Los Angeles Street. He parked in the mouth of the alley, blocking access. He wanted the car close.

The alley was dark. Sheets of windblown rain assured that he could see only a few feet in front of him. He estimated that he had gone about twenty-five feet into the alley. The trash cans should be close. He moved to his left.

"Hey, you!" The deep and loud voice came from his left.

Brian turned toward the sound. An unkempt, frail man came into view as if he had emerged from the wall. Brian's heart raced. He raised his hands in a defensive posture.

"What are you doing in my house?" the old man shouted.

Brian dropped his hands. It was just one of the locals feeling territorial. "You scared the shit out of me, mister."

It was as if the man didn't hear a word Brian had said. "Get out of my house."

The man looked ancient. It appeared that, if the wind blew any stronger, he would be blown off his feet.

"I'm sorry for the inconvenience, my friend." Brian pulled a ten-dollar bill from his wallet and handed it to the man.

The old man studied it closely and then looked at Brian. "It's okay. You can stay as long as you want." The man turned and walked away from him, cackling as he clutched the money.

Brian walked on and almost immediately saw the two garbage cans. He turned over the second can and found a large brown envelope, about a foot thick, taped to the bottom. He tore away the tape and held the envelope close to his midsection as he ran back to the car.

He threw the envelope in the back seat and spun the tires as he moved away from the alley. The day's events reeled around in his head. It was all beyond his control. Whatever decision he made, he was fucked. The parking ticket was the best thing that had happened all day, and things only promised to get worse. It suddenly occurred to him that he didn't have to be alone in all this; there was someone with the ability to help, a person he could trust.

When Brian got home, Barbara met him at the door. He walked in, and she threw her arms around him. "You okay?"

He nodded.

"What happened?" she pressed with an anxious expression on her face.

"I got what he sent me for."

He pulled the brown envelope from inside his soaked jacket. He opened the envelope and pulled out a large wad of paper. Brian worked his way to the center of it and pulled out a handgun. Barbara seemed to jump.

"Your basic Saturday night special," Brian mumbled in the direction of the gun.

"Let's take it to the police. They can trace it."

Brian shook his head. "This guy's no fool. This won't be traceable."

"So what now?" she asked, staring at the gun.

"We call Bob Galvin. He's the guy to help us."

She furrowed her brow. "Your private investigator buddy from your law firm days?"

Brian nodded. Bob had done some impressive work in helping Brian prepare his cases for trial. More than once, he had come up with evidence that had turned a case Brian's way. "Maybe Bob can check out this Jason Ross guy and who might want to kill him."

She nodded toward the phone. "What if he finds out?"

"He'll never know. Bob's real good at being invisible." He could see from her expression that the doubts were still there.

It was nine thirty when the phone rang again.

"Hello?" Brian said, even though he knew who was calling.

"You found the tool?" the deep voice asked.

"I found it," Brian said.

"Any questions?"

Brian had questions about all that had happened. There were no answers though. "No, I have no questions."

The man said, "I'll talk to you Tuesday night, Brian," and then there was a dial tone.

It was about six the next morning when Bob Galvin knocked on the door. Bob made a formidable appearance at six foot three and two twenty. He was broad shouldered and solid. The bulk was muscle without fat. His short blond hair, small nose, and rounded features made him look younger than his thirty-eight years. His sly grin enhanced the appearance of youth.

Brian pulled him in quickly and then closed the door. He gave his friend a hug. "How have you been, Bob?"

"I've been doing fine. Business is good these days. Everybody and their dog needs somebody found, followed, or served." He grinned in his own friendly way. "Haven't heard from you since your elevation to political prominence."

"I know, buddy, and I'm sorry. We should be drinking beer together from time to time."

"Yeah, and belching. You were always good at that. Can you still do it now that you're a congressman?"

"Better than ever. Now I have indigestion all the time." Brian laughed nervously.

"So what's going on, my friend? I have a feeling this isn't just social."

"No, it's not. I need your help."

Bob sat in the living room and listened as Brian told him about the death of Cathy Jenkins and the calls that had followed. He told Bob what happened with each call, the demand he kill Jason Ross, and the trip downtown to get the gun. Then he told Bob that he was being watched and that everything was to happen on Tuesday. He told Bob about all of it, except his relationship with Cathy. He was leaving that out again, still hoping that Barbara wouldn't have to know.

Bob asked questions and took notes. Brian answered most and avoided others, like why he didn't go straight to the police. Some of his answers lacked convincing force, and he knew Bob sensed it. Maybe later he would explain it all, but just not yet.

At seven thirty, Bob announced he had to do something but would return in half hour. As they walked out to the car, Brian saw Bob observe the surrounding houses, in search of some clue. He gave no indications of finding anything. Bob slid behind the wheel of his Jaguar, gave Brian a wave, and drove away. Brian walked back into the house to wait. He looked around for strange faces, unfamiliar cars, or the subtle movement of drapes. He saw nothing.

In forty-five minutes, Bob was pounding on the backdoor. Brian unlocked the door, and Bob came in carrying a large briefcase.

"You came in through the backyard?" Brian asked.

"Yeah. I parked a couple blocks away and came over a couple fences. Practicing being inconspicuous, you know. It comes with the job."

They walked into the living room, and Bob put the case down on the couch and opened it. It contained several electronic devices, each secured in indentations of soft foam the same shape as the object. Bob removed a short, wand-shaped device.

He turned a knob near its handle and then looked at Brian and smiled. "We'll see if we can find out how this guy knows what you're doing and whether you've called anyone."

Brian nodded and watched as Bob moved around the room with the device, paying particular attention to lampshades, vases, anything with crevices, or something that might serve as a container. It took him thirty minutes to slowly cover the entire house in this fashion.

When he was through, he looked at Brian and shook his head. "Nothing."

Bob then returned to the briefcase and took out another device, this one smaller than the first with a small gauge on its face. He flipped a switch, and a red light appeared on the base of the object. He then took the device to the telephone in the living room and pointed it at the receiver. There was no visible reaction on the gauge. He walked around the house again, repeating the procedure with each of the four telephones.

The result was always the same. Bob put the device back in the case and looked at Brian. "The good news is that you still have your privacy. The bad news is that I didn't find any clues to help me identify this guy."

Brian looked at him quizzically. "You can find him from a listening device?"

"Yeah, sometimes. I can trace the device. I have some contacts inside the industry I can call on to find out who bought what."

Brian nodded, impressed at his friend's abilities.

"Doesn't help us much this time," Bob said sadly.

Barbara walked into the room at that moment. "I'm glad to hear it. I don't want to think that this creep is listening to the intimate details of our lives."

Bob nodded. "I can understand that. This may be one sick puppy we've got here."

"So what now?" Brian asked.

"Now we have coffee," Bob said. "I need a jump-start before I go looking for this crazy asshole."

Barbara smiled. "Yeah, let's go in the kitchen. A fresh pot is brewing. We've got some coffee cake too. You interested?"

"I'm interested." Bob stood quickly. "I'll have to put you guys on my regular breakfast circuit."

* * *

As they finished a second cup of coffee and Bob had eaten his second piece of coffee cake, Bob shook his head. "Damn, this is good stuff. Looks like an extra hour at the gym to pay for this one."

They laughed as he slapped himself on an imagined belly.

Bob checked his watch. "Well, time to get down to business, my friends."

Bob hugged Barbara and then Brian. "It's good to see you guys. Been too long."

"It's good to see you too, Bob," Barbara said. "I had forgotten what a likable character you are."

"Aw shucks, ma'am," he said, pretending to tip his hat to her.

"Well, at least until we get to the John Wayne stuff," she said, and they laughed again.

Brian returned the conversation to more serious tones. "You think you can figure out who's doing this?"

Bob nodded. "It's probably someone who's no stranger to Jason Ross. People usually don't care about strangers enough to want to kill them."

"Probably?" Brian asked.

"Yeah, we can't rule out anything. We have a stranger calling you to get you to murder someone you don't know. Maybe some other stranger called him."

"Like some sort of a murder pyramid scheme?"

"Something like that, or maybe a professional job. Perhaps this is a contract and our man isn't real close to Ross at all."

"That's crazy!" Brian exclaimed.

"Damn straight. The whole deal is crazy. All I'm saying is that we can't rule anything out yet."

"I understand," Brian said more calmly.

"But this Ross guy is a good place to start. I'll check into his family and career and see what turns up. I'll call you as soon as I have anything."

Brian thanked Bob as he picked up his equipment and walked out the backdoor, again practicing being inconspicuous.

* * *

The private line rang twice and then stopped. Fifteen seconds later, it rang again. Michael picked it up on the third ring.

"Yeah?" He listened intently and then sat back in his chair. "Oh, shit." There was silence. Then he said, "We really have no choice." The voice spoke again, and Michael replied in anger, "No fucking way! I'm not doing that."

The voice on the phone was calm and deliberate. "If you've got a better idea, I'd love to hear it."

There was silence while Michael ran a hand through his hair.

"We have no choice. Think about it." The voice on the phone was detached and logical.

Michael calmed himself and then spoke again, "I'll take care of it. Talk to you tomorrow."

He hung up the phone and let out a soft whistle. He knew that every new variable increased the risk. Everything was in motion, and there was no longer a way back, like free falling before the parachute is pulled. After the first step, there was no turning back—no matter how fast you fall, no matter how close the ground gets, and no matter if the parachute doesn't open.

He stood and walked to the closed door of his office. He opened the door quietly and looked out, just to be sure. Sheila was busily engaged on the computer. Michael closed the door and walked over to the window. There was little time to think.

Chapter 9

After twenty-five years of investigating everything from missing executives to disloyal spouses, Bob was good at what he did. He liked having the chance to help an old friend in trouble. It felt worthwhile, even if there were things his friend wasn't telling him, even if there weren't much to work with yet.

As he drove north toward his house in Gold Hills, Bob reflected on his conversation with Brian or, more accurately, the things Brian hadn't told him. There was something more that Brian knew but wasn't telling him about how he got dragged into all of this. There were always things that friends kept from one another, and that was usually okay, except in his business. Bob had learned a long time ago that what he didn't know was the most likely to get the shit kicked out of him or worse. Hopefully, he would talk Brian into telling him the rest of it sooner rather than later. He sensed that whatever he had withheld had been based on Barbara's presence. Bob would have to speak to his friend alone, let him know that he needed the missing parts, and affirm that he wouldn't tell Barbara. Then he would learn more.

In the meantime, he was working on the missing pieces. It had something to do with money, a bad business deal, or a woman. It almost always did. Bob had already called into the office and put his secretary to work on learning as much as possible about

Jason Ross. Within a half hour, she had called him back with the basics, the identity and descriptions of family members and business associates. He knew what Ross did for a living and whom he did it for. He was a heavyweight at International Resource. He was a good choice for a target. *Money and power*, Bob thought.

Bob pulled into his driveway and climbed out of the Jaguar. He walked up the driveway, stopping to grab the mail from the pelican-shaped mailbox by the curb. He loved the sea and vowed that one day he would live within steps of it. Until then he would have to settle for distant images like seagull refrigerator magnets and a pelican-shaped mailbox. He stopped momentarily to listen to the sounds of birds singing out their greetings as they jumped between branches. He smiled at the spring scene and the beautiful day and then walked up to the door.

He unlocked the door and walked into the house, distracted by the envelopes in his hand. He looked up just in time to see a man standing in the hallway. The man pointed something at him, and before Bob could move, he felt the jolt as the electricity coursed through his body. The sudden pain was followed by an overwhelming blackness as Bob fell to the floor.

* * *

At noon, Brian sat in his office, feeling renewed confidence now that Bob was on his side. He made notes on the Senate legislation that would require insurance companies to reimburse premiums when profit levels were deemed unconscionable.

The short, sharp sound of the intercom caught him off guard. "Yes," he said curtly into the speakerphone.

"There's a man on the phone who won't give his name, but he says you'll know who he is and you'll want to talk to him. Shall I tell him you're unavailable?"

Brian's voice cracked as he forced a response. "I'll take it. Thanks."

Brian stared at the phone for a moment, taking several deep breaths to calm himself. He snatched up the phone. "Brian Madsen here."

"You betrayed me." Brian knew the voice. This time it was angry.

"What do you mean?" Brian asked nervously.

"You betrayed your friend Bob. I told you not to talk to anyone, Brian. Now you've hurt your friend."

"Oh my God." Brian involuntarily put a hand over his mouth and leaned forward in his chair. "What have you done to him?"

There was a pause. When the man spoke, it was in measured, angry tones. "Apparently you haven't taken me seriously, Brian. I've been trying to help you avoid murder charges, remember? Maybe I'll just send all the evidence to the police now and we'll be done talking. Maybe you'd rather face the death penalty than cooperate. Is that your decision?"

"What have you done to Bob?" Brian raised his voice, but it signaled more panic than anger.

"He's no longer able to help you. No one is. You have a choice to make. It's real simple. Are you ready to do what I ask, or do you want to do more damage?"

Brian was silent. He was desperately scared. His thoughts raced. *Could I really kill someone to get out of this mess? Or should I just admit to everything and try to convince everyone that I didn't kill Cathy? Convince them with what?* he thought. *Our secret affair? My fingerprints on everything in her apartment, maybe even the murder weapon in the possession of this terrorist?* He had nothing that would convince anyone of his innocence. *How could I kill someone? Someone I didn't even know? Because a voice on the telephone demanded it?*

"Still not sure, Brian? Try to contact Bob. Then listen to the news tonight, and you'll know that all I'm telling you is real." The line went dead.

* * *

At two o'clock, Michael Hayward stared out the window of his office. Twice during the past two days, he had called Jason Ross, the first time offering his congratulations and the second time his full cooperation. He had followed up the visits with a lengthy email, updating Ross on pending projects and suggesting strategies on each. He was smiling, amused by Jason Ross' confusion at being treated with so much accommodation and respect.

Sheila buzzed him. "Mike, your wife is on line two."

"Thanks, Sheila." He slapped at the button. "Hi, Carol."

"Mike, don't forget the Largent's party tonight. You need to get home in time for us to leave by seven."

"No problem. I'll be there."

"You sound like you're in good spirits today."

"Yeah, I am." His grin widened.

"What happened to all that anger about the promotion?"

"I guess I just figured out that the anger was counterproductive. Besides, I think Jason and I are going to work things out. Being number-two man will come with plenty of clout."

"That's good news, Mike. I'm glad."

He looked out at the sea of movement thirty-five stories below. "Everything's going to be fine."

"So I'll see you at about six thirty?"

"You will. Bye, Carol."

Michael put the telephone back in its cradle and turned to see Sheila standing in the open doorway, looking at him quizzically. "You've worked things out with Jason Ross?" she asked suspiciously.

Michael was momentarily caught off guard. For just a second, he knew that his expression gave it away. Then he regained his poise. "I'm hopeful that we will. Nothing has been finalized yet."

She stood there in silence and then said, "I'm just surprised."

He nodded, now in full control once again. "I've thought about it a great deal. I've concluded that sometimes you have to make the best of a little less than what you wanted. This is one of those times."

She nodded her approval. "That's a great attitude. I just wouldn't have guessed you'd arrive there." Her thoughts returned to the reason she had come into the office, and she asked him a question about a proposed board resolution.

Michael smiled as he gave her direction. He really did feel good.

* * *

Brian had not been able to reach Bob all afternoon, as had been promised. A half-dozen messages were unreturned. Bob's office had no idea where he was, but his secretary said it wasn't unusual for him to get caught up in an assignment for longer than anticipated. He would call in by tomorrow morning at the latest.

At five o'clock, Brian turned on the local news. "Good evening, ladies and gentlemen," said a suave-looking man in his mid-forties. He wore a blue suit and sat behind a desk staring into the camera. "Our top story tonight is breaking news in the murder case of International Resource Corporation Marketing Manager Cathy Jenkins. We are informed that tomorrow's *Los Angeles Times* will report that the victim had sexual intercourse shortly before her murder. It will also be reported that the intercourse was consensual. There is no evidence of rape or sexual molestation."

Brian could feel his stomach muscles tightening.

"This is consistent with the present police theory that Ms. Jenkins knew her assailant and let him into her home voluntarily."

Just hearing it made Brian feel more nauseated. With every news release, the inevitable seemed close. It would all come back to him.

"In a second development on the case, the police received a jewelry box this afternoon, which family members have already confirmed as belonging to the victim. It is in police laboratories tonight for analysis. Police are hopeful that this new piece of evidence will provide some clue as to the identity of the killer. Police are not saying how they obtained the jewelry box, but apparently it is just one of a number of belongings that were removed from the scene on the night of the murder. We will keep you informed of all late-breaking events in connection with this tragedy. In other news tonight, there have been seventeen arrests in connection with the city's biggest drug bust in—"

Brian pushed the power button of the remote, and the set fell silent. Cathy had loved that jewelry box. He had watched her glow as she made the ballerina twirl to the music. He had touched the music box several times to turn it on for her, to watch her light up. Sergeant Merrick would be back soon with more questions, to have Brian repeat his denials that he saw her socially. And he'd have a warrant for his arrest. It was all so out of control. Brian stood and ran to the bathroom. He lifted the toilet seat and threw up.

Chapter 10

Brian stayed awake all night. He paced, he stared out the living room window into the darkness, and he turned on a Godzilla movie that no one was supposed to be awake to see at three in the morning. Actors with strong Japanese accents spoke English words, dubbed in over Japanese dialogue. The loud roar of the monster preceded the movement of its mouth by about three seconds.

After fifteen minutes of halfheartedly listening to prehistoric growling and watching buildings being flattened and insignificantly small humans fleeing with their hands in the air, Brian returned to bed. Barbara asked if he were okay. By the time he mumbled that he was, she had already fallen back to sleep, if she had really been awake. Brian stared at the ceiling and thought about Cathy. He wished he could talk to her one more time, to find out what happened that night and to tell her that he cared.

He drifted off to sleep and saw the jewelry box and Cathy's laughing eyes watching it joyfully as the ballerina danced. Then he saw Cathy standing in front of him in a long, flowing dress that imperceptible breeze moved. Love filled her blue eyes. She reached out to Brian. He smiled and reached out to take her hands. He found that she was just out of reach. She was still smiling at him, still beckoning. A veil of fog surrounded her, and Brian found it hard to see. Then she began to move backward, away from him. She extended her arms to reach for him, and then she was gone.

Brian awoke, sitting up with his arms extended in darkness. He stared out into the dark room and waited. There was only silence. The dream had been so real. He wiped a tear from his eye and climbed out of bed. He walked to the front door and looked out. *Nothing.*

He went into the kitchen and poured a glass of water. Then he sat down at the kitchen table to wait. By now the police would have what they needed from the jewelry box, and they would be coming. Merrick would soon knock on the door. Brian wondered if he should wake up Barbara to tell her before they got there. He got as far as the bedroom door before stopping. He watched her sleep, at peace in a world far away, and he couldn't do it. He returned to the kitchen table and sat down to wait. Every few minutes he went to the front door to look out. At morning's first light, Brian still waited. The knock never came.

At seven a.m., Brian sat in the dining room, drinking coffee. Barbara was still asleep. The telephone rang. He picked it up before it rang again.

"Brian?" the killer said in an ominous voice.

"Yeah, this is Brian."

"I trust you saw the news?"

"I saw it."

"The object is clean. I made sure of it. No prints, no hair, and no fibers. Understand?"

Brian audibly let out a breath of air with the sudden relief. He felt a perverse gratitude toward this monster that made him feel sick. "I understand." Brian hesitated. "A warning."

"Yes. So that you know, I could have left your name written all over it. And if I need to, I will."

"I see," Brian said with resignation.

"Do you? You touched many things in her apartment, Brian. Maybe that box of condoms you kept in the nightstand will be

83

next. Not only will they know you were there, they'll know who Ms. Jenkins was sleeping with, right?" The man paused for effect. "Did you let them know that you knew her intimately? It'll be hard to explain the condoms if you didn't. Or maybe we should get right to the key object. Give them the so-called smoking gun. What do you think?"

"You son of a bitch," Brian hissed.

"Expressing your anger to someone else may be good therapy, but don't waste it on me. I don't want this to happen, I've told you that before. I just want your cooperation."

"I know what you want."

"Today is Tuesday. Is it going to happen?"

Brian wiped the sweat from his forehead. "Oh, God, I don't know. I just don't know."

"Okay, I've done what I can to convince you. I'm running out of patience." The line went dead.

Brian put down the telephone, feeling on the verge of panic. It was hard to catch his breath, and his eyes were beginning to tear. The tears were misting in his eyes, blurring his vision. *If only he could really kill this Ross, it could be all over.* He almost wanted to, just to buy some peace, but he didn't think he could do it. If he had a chance though, he would kill that son of a bitch on the telephone.

Brian put his head in his hands. He needed to compose himself and consider all the options one more time. He still couldn't go to the police. There was another solution, and it shocked him that it would even occur to him. For a passing moment, Brian thought about taking his own life. He knew he wouldn't do that either. He sat with his head in his hands, feeling scared and alone. Then he did something he hadn't done in a long time. He prayed for help.

At nine o'clock, Brian kissed Barbara good-bye and left for the office. He was without sleep and not sure how much he could accomplish, but some things couldn't be postponed. Maybe he was just clinging to the few remnants of normalcy that remained in his life. He knew it wouldn't last. Fear paralyzed him into inaction. He was making no decision about Jason Ross' future or his own. And he had no time.

Brian told himself he couldn't kill a stranger in a parking lot. This was a man who probably had a family and a career, a life. Brian didn't think he could do it, even to keep himself away from murder charges or to save his marriage. And God help him, not even to help Bob, wherever he was. Brian couldn't stop the caller from doing whatever he was going to do. So there was nothing to do but wait for the inevitable, for his house of cards to fall.

Brian spent the morning returning calls and preparing for a policy formulation meeting with Congressman Wilson Shaw and party chairman Byron Epstein, important men in the same party who just happened to be natural enemies. Brian was going to negotiate proposed party policies with two men who couldn't agree on what day it was while they were staring at a calendar and who were guaranteed to be raising voices at one another before the salutations were over. Brian only hoped they wouldn't bring weapons. At least planning the meeting was a momentary distraction from the weight of the thoughts that seemed to overwhelm his mind during every waking hour.

At ten o'clock, he called Barbara to make sure everything was okay. The phone rang three times before she answered, and Brian found himself more nervous with each ring.

"Hello?" she said.

"You okay, Barb?" Brian asked quickly.

"Yeah, I'm okay. I guess. It's all pretty eerie though, you know?"

"Yeah, I know."

"I'm going to get out of the house for a while. Janet's coming over with Lindsay, and we're going to do a couple chores and then go to lunch."

Brian was glad. Janet was more than a sister to Barbara. She was a good friend. He was sure Barbara could use someone to talk to right now.

"Sounds like a great idea. Give her my love, will you?"

"I will."

"And tell Lindsay her Uncle Brian plans to tickle her senseless."

"I'll do that. I can already hear her giggling."

"Call me when you get back and we'll plan dinner."

"Sounds good. I love you, Brian."

"I love you too." As Brian put down the phone, he thought about the fact that neither of them had spoken of the caller or about the fact that it was Tuesday.

* * *

Bob began to regain consciousness. Everything was fuzzy. It was dark, and he was lying on his stomach, unable to move. His hands were tied behind him, and his legs were bound together at the ankles. He could feel the tightly drawn cloth of the blindfold over his eyes and another piece of cloth over his mouth. Slowly the haze began to clear. He remembered the ambush at his home. He remembered some kind of a stun gun. Then nothing until now. He had no idea how much time had passed.

Bob tugged at the bindings on his wrists and ankles. There was not much give. He relaxed and tried to collect his thoughts. For all he knew, his abductor was just a few feet away. He had to go slowly. He rolled to his right and hit a wall only a foot away. He rolled to his left and hit something soft. He rolled into it again and realized it was clothing. He pushed harder and felt a hard surface beyond the fabric. He was in a closet of some kind. The way he was bound and isolated probably meant his captor was not nearby.

Bob began to work his jaw to try to free himself of the bindings. He flexed and extended his hands and wrists, trying to find some give in the rope. He knew he had his work cut out for him. What he didn't know was how much time he had before someone returned.

After pulling at the ropes for about twenty minutes with little progress, Bob devised an alternative. He rolled to the door and then crawled to bring himself into alignment with the jamb. He began rubbing the ropes that bound his wrists against the sharp edge of the hinge. His movement was limited, so the process yielded minimal progress and maximal exertion. As he applied pressure to his bindings, Bob began a mental review of his cases in an effort to identify his captor. It didn't take long to conclude that the possibilities were numerous.

Chapter 11

Barbara pulled up to the curb and looked toward the blue and white, single-story house near the end of the cul-de-sac. Janet and Lindsay came out waving and walked toward the car. Lindsay's had pulled her long brown hair back and flowing down below her shoulders. Her bangs pointed the way to big, brown eyes that sparkled alternatively with intelligence and curiosity. Her small turned-up nose and ear-to-ear smile made her irresistible.

Barbara waved and waited as Janet opened the door and climbed in the front. Janet had the same jet-black hair as Barbara, but she wore it short, and it curled under at her shoulders. Her hazel eyes seemed to hold an expression of cynicism. She had the same high cheekbones as Barbara and moved with the same elegance.

"Hi, Jan," she said.

"Hey, sis, what's new? Other than your whole lifestyle, that is."

Barbara nodded. "You've got that right. Life changes rather abruptly when you're suddenly married to a Congressman." She looked in the back seat and got a big grin from Lindsay. "Hi, Aunt Barbara." She leaned forward in the seat and reached out to give Barbara a hug.

Barbara touched her cheek and smiled. "So how's my favorite niece?"

Lindsay shook her head and frowned. "I'm your only niece." She looked rather seriously at Barbara, waiting for this important point to register.

Barbara nodded. "I didn't mean favorite of my nieces. I mean my favorite of everybody's nieces."

Lindsay chuckled. "In that case," she said quite seriously, "can we get some popcorn to go with the movie?"

"Is there any other way?" Barbara asked as she turned and shifted the car into drive.

"No," came the giggled response from the back seat.

Barbara looked up to find Janet staring at her. "What? Did I violate some rule of driving etiquette?" Barbara asked.

"Not yet," her sister said without a hint of humor.

"Then what is it?"

"I just think you're so good with kids that you should have a few of your own."

"A few? Like a litter or something?"

Lindsay was giggling again.

"Maybe. There's a lot of wasted talent here."

Barbara frowned. "Now there's a nice left-handed compliment."

"No, I mean it. You have so much to offer a child. You and Brian would be great parents." Janet furrowed her brow. "I mean, don't you want to have kids?"

Barbara stared straight ahead, thinking of what to say. *Yeah, I have wanted kids for the past ten years. I wanted to know what it felt like to have a beautiful, innocent child call me Mom and ask for a hug.*

"Barb?" Janet said after a moment.

"Sorry. I was just thinking for a minute. Yeah, I want kids." Barbara paused. "But you may have noticed that we're a little busy at this point in our lives."

Janet nodded. "So what are you going to do, put it off until right after menopause?"

"Dammit, Janet, must you be so damned blunt," Barbara said indignantly.

"Ummmmm." The sound came from the back seat. Barbara knew what it was about. "Aunt Barbara, you swore."

"Sorry, sweetheart. I guess it just slipped out," Barbara said more calmly.

Lindsay still had a serious face on. "You did it twice, you know."

"Well, I'm sorry for both times."

"Okay." Barbara could see Lindsay's face in the rearview mirror, now satisfied. "Are we almost there?"

"Not yet, Lindsay. But soon."

"So you never answered my blunt question," Janet said.

"I know. Some people would get the message."

"Maybe. But not sisters."

Barbara shook her head in exasperation. "No, I don't want to wait until I stop ovulating. Yes, I want kids, all right?"

"All right. When?"

Barbara grimaced. "What? Are you scheduling the delivery room?"

"No, I just think it's time my little sister made me an aunt too. Turn right at the next corner," Janet said, pointing.

"I know where Hometown Video is. We go there too."

"Really? The wife of a Congressman? Isn't there someone you can send?"

"Oh, we're real funny today," Barbara said, sarcastically.

There was a brief silence while Barbara thought about her answer. Janet knew she would think it through and reply. Lindsay was bored.

"Maybe after we get settled in Washington, you know." There was no audible response, and Barbara didn't turn to look at

Janet's expression. "Right now, our life is pretty nuts; meeting people everywhere for dinners and parties. The whole bit."

Janet nodded silently. It was the nod of someone who thought she knew something and a nod Barbara found annoying.

"All right. What?" she finally said.

"I didn't say anything."

"I know, that's the point. Whatever you didn't say is written all over your face. Like you know something the rest of us don't."

"My, aren't we in a mood?" Janet said haughtily.

"We weren't, but we may be getting there. Just say it, Janet."

"I just think all this being busy shit is just an excuse."

"Mom!" Lindsay exclaimed.

"Sorry, honey."

Barbara was momentarily caught off guard. She knew it showed in her expression. "Meaning?"

"Meaning life is always busy. Kids just come along anyway."

Barbara nodded. That rang true, and it pushed her buttons. Janet always had a way of getting to the heart of a wound. The salt was never added intentionally. She was just so direct.

Janet saw Barbara's pained expression and decided to lighten the conversation with a little humor. "Besides, Brian's a good-looking guy. Smart, witty, and connected. This overwhelming success is a good opportunity to see if he can resist all the women who want to throw themselves at him." She chuckled, but the response wasn't what she expected. She could see Barbara tensing up.

"Is that supposed to be funny?" Barbara asked through clenched teeth.

The anger took Janet by surprise. "Yeah, it was." There was a momentary silence. Then Janet asked, "Is there something going on with you and Brian that you want to share?"

"No," Barbara said coldly.

"I'm sorry, Barb. I really didn't mean anything by it."

"I know," she said, sighing. "I'm sorry I lost it. There's just a lot of pressure right now and ..." Her voice trailed off. For a fleeting moment, she had almost said too much. She pulled into the plaza.

With recognition of the video store, Lindsay let out a squeal of delight. "We're here!"

Janet smiled at her daughter. "Yes, we are, sweetheart. Let's go choose a funny movie and some popcorn."

Her innocent little face lit up with excitement, and Barbara's heart hurt with a sense of loss.

They climbed out of the car, and Lindsay ran on ahead. Janet put her arm around Barbara, and they followed Lindsay's exuberant footfalls toward the store. There were posters of movies available and those soon to come, covering the all-glass front of the store.

Lindsay stood at the window, pointing toward a poster as they approached her. They were within ten feet of the store when a horrible blast from behind them broke the afternoon silence. Before they could turn to see, the concussion lifted them from their feet and thrust them at the building. The blast tore apart the store windows and hurled glass projectiles in all directions. The force of the blast thrust Barbara into what was left of the window, shards of glass tearing at her body. Pieces of wood and metal that used to be the building's trim flew through the air. There were remnants of movie posters, now nothing more than charred scraps of paper floating on the breeze.

Barbara landed on the wooden floor of what used to be the store. She landed on her left shoulder, dazed. Some time passed, although she had no idea how long. Slowly she became aware of her surroundings. She looked around her. The windows and pieces of the overhanging roof were gone. Flames and smoke were coming from the parking lot.

"Hey, lady, you okay?" She could barely hear the unfamiliar male voice.

The sounds came to her slowly, and it took some time for Barbara to comprehend the words. She realized she was nodding to the stranger. She looked around for Lindsay and Janet, but could see neither of them. She tried to make it to her feet.

"Take it easy, lady. You shouldn't get up yet." It was the same voice.

"Help me up. I have to find my sister and my niece. Where's Lindsay? She's just seven. Please find her." Barbara felt weak, like her legs might not hold her upright. The stranger put his arms around her and helped her to a chair. "What about my sister and my niece?" Barbara cried.

"Your sister looks okay. I'm not sure about the little girl, but she's being helped, and an ambulance is on the way."

"Where are they?" Barbara knew she was yelling.

The man pointed across what was left of the room. She could see them. Janet was kneeling on the floor, looking down. Something was in Barbara's eye. She raised a hand to clear it away, and her hand came back red. She looked at the blood and wondered where it had come from. She couldn't feel anything. Running her hand over her face, she found the cut on her forehead. She called out to Lindsay and Janet and then began to move toward them. Lindsay's small figure was motionless. Barbara kneeled down next to Janet and looked at her sister's face.

"You okay?" she asked Janet.

Janet's arms and face were cut and bleeding, but she didn't seem to notice. She was crying and squeezing Lindsay's hand.

"She's not moving," Janet said hysterically. "My baby's not moving."

Barbara looked down at Lindsay's still figure. A stranger held a blood-soaked towel against her neck. Blood seeped from under the towel. An open wound was on Lindsay's forehead. A piece of glass protruded from her forearm. Barbara leaned toward Lindsay and could tell her breathing was shallow. The parts of her face that weren't bloody had turned ghostly white.

There were sirens outside, and police officers began to arrive.

Two officers ran over to them. "It's okay, ma'am," one of them said as he put his arm around Barbara and helped her to a chair. "Let's give the paramedics some working room. They'll help her."

She could only nod. She could see Janet being helped by the other officer, and she could hear her sister's voice calling out in pain, "My baby. Please help my baby. Don't let her die."

Barbara felt the room spinning. Outside, she could see what was left of her car, consumed by flames. She sat helplessly amongst the rubble of the shop, saying a prayer for Lindsay.

Chapter 12

Brian sat in the conference room with Congressmen Shaw and Epstein. Shaw and Epstein sat at opposing ends of the eight-foot conference table. Epstein took long sips from his black coffee. Brian sat near the middle of the table, the mediator between warring nations.

One wall of the conference room was all glass that looked out onto a triangular atrium. One of the walls was taken up by bookshelves, filled to capacity and the other two walls were decorated with historical shots of the capital building.

"This is not the right time for rhetoric based on spending," the congressional representative said, lighting a cigar the size of a small umbrella. Shaw's thick, white hair pushed backward like it was fleeing his face was a feature that many thought gave him a look of dignity and sophistication. He wore a blue jacket over white slacks that worked hard to contain the stomach that spilled over his belt.

Rather than political worldliness, Brian envisioned a picture of Shaw over a caption that asked whether you would buy a used car from this man. To Brian, the answer would be a resounding "no."

Shaw looked around the room, allowing his words of wisdom to settle on his audience. He leaned back in the chair as he blew out a ring of smoke. Brian looked at his watch for the third time in as many minutes, wishing it were later than two thirty and waiting for the other shoe to drop.

"We have an abundance of rhetoric about saving taxpayer dollars in the party policy already," Epstein said. "Somewhere along the way, John Q. Public is going to want to know what we're spending his money on. Let's tell him something to convince him he's getting some return. I don't care what: defense, cops on the street, or unwed mothers of elderly AIDS patients with homeless cousins. You pick it. Only we have to have something to tell the voters other than we're not going to spend."

Characteristically, Epstein was perturbed. He was a behind-the-scenes career man who saw politicians come and go over his twenty-five years in the arena and didn't like most of them, Shaw even more so than most. Epstein brushed a hand over his hairless head and down to the bearded chin that seemed to hide his small mouth. He was a man who kept himself in good shape with regular workouts and a good diet, two more reasons not to like Shaw. His unwelcome cigar smoke perpetually filled every room he occupied without regard for anyone of equal or lower rank, and he was out-of-control fat.

"Mr. Epstein, the voters elected myself and Congressman Madsen here," Shaw said as he waved a hand at Brian, "to protect them from the excess of government, not to find new ways to spend their money. Am I right, Brian?"

Both men looked at Brian. He felt like a referee in a cockfight. Brian looked at each of the men, resisting the urge to tell them to drop their pants so he could measure and declare a winner. His thoughts were torn between these adolescents and what was about to happen to his life. The significance of the former was hard to find under the circumstances.

He looked first at Shaw. "I think Bryan's right, Congressman. I think we have to tell people what our programs are and not just what they aren't."

Then he looked at Epstein. "And I think you should stop being such a hard ass. If the congressional representative wants to toss in some more bullshit about how frugal the party is, what the fuck? There's no downside, is there?" Brian's no-more-bullshit pronouncement visibly shocked Epstein.

When Brian looked back at the smoky visage of Congressman Shaw, he was smiling, obviously delighted with Brian's comments. Brian had no idea why he should delight in the characterization of his rhetoric as bullshit.

Brian frowned. "And you know what, Congressman. I don't remember inviting you to poison us all with that exhaust pipe you're sucking on."

Shaw's expression immediately changed to anger, and for a moment, it appeared he would walk out. Epstein, never the poker player, sat there with his mouth open. Brian sat back and waited, not caring what happened. Weightier thoughts consumed him.

Shaw stared at him for several moments and then broke into loud laughter. He put out the cigar and slapped Brian on the shoulder. "Goddamn, boy. You are one ballsy son of a bitch, you know? I knew we got us a good one here."

Epstein began to grin.

"Okay, Brian," Shaw said grudgingly, "so we tell them where some money's going. Only shit that everybody wants though. You know, tough laws and cops. No minority programs. Nothing that's going to piss off half of my constituents even before we do it."

Brian gave him a hard look. "Okay, Congressman, so partial disclosure of what we're spending and how much we're saving by not disclosing where the other money goes, is that it?" There was a knock at the door. "Come in," Brian said, not sorry for the interruption.

Trudy Miller, his newly hired staff assistant, stood in the doorway looking nervously at Brian. "I'm sorry to interrupt,

Mr. Madsen, but you have an emergency call on line three. It's the police."

Brian nodded. He wasn't surprised. It had only been a matter of time. He stood and looked at Epstein and Shaw. "Excuse me, gentlemen. Please continue." He turned toward his nervous assistant. "Thanks, Trudy. I'll take it in my office."

As Brian walked to the phone, he mused over how resigned he was to the situation, the emergency that he accepted so matter-of-factly. He was only surprised that they weren't at the office to arrest him. Brian walked into his office and sat behind the desk. He watched the blinking light for a few seconds, a short reprieve before all hell broke loose.

He picked up the receiver and pushed the flashing button. "Brian Madsen here."

"Mr. Madsen, this is Officer Jackson." The voice was young and serious. "There's been an accident, and your family was involved."

Brian's heart raced as he thought of Barbara. "What happened?" he asked in a choked voice.

"There was an explosion outside a video store. I think you better come on over here."

"Where?"

"Hometown Video. Carlson and Santa Barbara. You know it?"

"Yes. I'll be there in ten minutes." Brian hung up and ran for the door. "I've got an emergency. I've got to go," he shouted.

He spoke to everyone and no one, not waiting for a response. He thought of the threatening voice on the telephone and what the man must have done. Brian prayed that they were all right. He had to do something to make this madness stop.

Brian raced into the plaza that housed Hometown Video, narrowly missing several people who stood transfixed. The plaza was in chaos. The façade of the video store had been blown apart. Glass, brick, and debris covered the parking lot. Smoke filled the air, and firemen hosed the remnants of Barbara's car to put out the last of the flames. Four police cars were stopped randomly in front of the scene, along with two fire engine companies.

"Oh my God. Please let them be okay. Don't let him have gotten to them," Brian moaned.

He leaped from the car in time to see one of the police cars moving away. An ambulance followed behind it. Through its window, he saw Barbara. She sat upright, wearing a bandage around her head and looking down. Brian glanced around as he moved toward the building.

"I'm sorry, sir. No closer," a uniformed officer told Brian, raising his arms to serve as a barrier.

"I'm Brian Madsen. My family's in there."

"Yes, sir," the officer said, lowering his arms. "See Officer Jackson near the front door." He pointed to Jackson, who turned and began walking toward Brian.

Jackson was a young black man with a rounded face and a solemn expression. "Mr. Madsen?"

"Yes. Where are they?" Brian asked.

"They were just taken to Inter-Community Medical Center."

Brian was shaking. "Are they okay?"

"I don't know, sir. They were all taken by ambulance a short time ago. The little girl was unconscious when they left."

Brian nodded and opened his mouth to speak. The shock had hit, and nothing would come out. He turned and ran for the car.

Brian arrived at the hospital to see Barbara standing in the emergency room. A sling immobilized her left arm and shoulder. Blood smeared her torn blouse.

"Brian," she called out to him across the large room. Then she waited for him to reach her. She threw her good arm around his neck and held on tightly.

"Barbara, are you all right?" he asked, nearly crying himself.

She nodded. "Just cuts and bruises and a fractured shoulder." She pointed to the sling. "Janet's cut up pretty badly, but she'll be okay. It's Lindsay that no one's sure about. She won't wake up, and her blood pressure is way down. She has some internal injuries and is in severe shock." She burst into tears. "They don't know if she'll make it, Brian. She's just a little girl. She hasn't even lived yet."

She leaned into Brian's shoulder and sobbed. He held her as closely as her injuries would permit and told her everything would be okay. Brian's stomach knotted. It didn't feel like everything would be okay, but he would do anything he could to buy Barbara some comfort.

* * *

Brian and Barbara sat in the hospital visitor's lounge, waiting for word on Janet and Lindsay. Brian looked at his watch. Two hours had passed. It was hard waiting, not knowing. Brian's thoughts moved between Lindsay's condition and the explosion to the voice on the telephone and his own protracted silence. He felt like a prisoner. He looked at Barbara. He smiled at her in an attempt to provide comfort to the pained expression on her face. She squeezed his hand.

The room was softly lit. Whatever the desired effect, it didn't work. It only served to add to the feeling of gloom that pervaded the hospital. Three others sat in this subdued light, waiting impatiently for some word on their personal pending disasters. As Brian looked around the room, the door burst open, and two police officers came in, one in street clothes and the other in uniform. A sudden discomfort accompanied recognition of the two. They walked directly over to Brian.

"Brian Madsen?" The deep voice came from the older man in slacks and a plaid shirt.

"Yes," Brian said uneasily.

"You remember me? I'm Sergeant Merrick. This is Officer Palmer."

The young, uniformed officer nodded abruptly, maintaining his trademark silence.

"I remember both of you. A police visit to my house is not a frequent occurrence." As Brian said it, he thought about how that might soon change.

Merrick nodded. "I need to ask you a couple questions. Please excuse the timing, but the sooner we put the pieces together, the better our chances are of finding who we're after."

"Okay, but me first. None of my questions have been answered either."

Merrick looked at him for a moment and then nodded. "Okay, go ahead."

"What happened out there? What have you learned about all this?" Brian asked, barely controlling his voice.

"Your family was walking from the car to the video store. Near as we can figure, they had almost made it to the front door when it all happened."

"When what happened?"

"When the car they were driving exploded. You saw what happened to the building."

"The explosive was in the car?" Brian asked, stunned.

"Yes, sir."

"Oh, Jesus."

Merrick acknowledged Brian's reaction with a nod. His expression was one of worry. "That was your wife's car, right?"

"Huh? Yeah, that was her Volvo." Brian's head felt heavy, and he let it fall to his hands.

Merrick stared at Brian. "You got any ideas about who might want to blow up your family?" Merrick asked.

Brian felt like he had been gut punched. He wanted to fall to the floor screaming. He knew exactly who had done this, and he knew nothing would stop him. He made himself find the words. "No one would want to hurt Barbara, Officer. Everybody loves her."

Merrick nodded. Then he pulled out a small spiral notebook and wrote for a moment. "How about her sister or the child? Anyone after them? Any domestic problems?"

Brian shook his head. "No, nothing."

As he finished speaking, a doctor, clad in hospital greens and matching cap, came into the room and walked toward them. "Barbara Madsen?" the young man said, looking at her.

"Yes," she said anxiously.

They all looked at the doctor expectantly.

He noticed the officers and gave them a nod of acknowledgment before continuing. "Your sister is okay. She has a couple of fractured ribs. Otherwise, just multiple bruises and abrasions that aren't serious. We'll have her out of here in two or three days."

Barbara nodded. "How about Lindsay? Is she okay?"

"To tell you the truth, we're not sure yet. She has fractures of the collarbone and a severe concussion. The biggest problem is that she's just not coming around yet and the next forty-eight hours are critical. She's getting nourishment intravenously, and she's being constantly monitored. There's just not much more we can do at this point."

Brian saw Barbara tearing up as she said, "I understand, doctor. Thanks." She was quiet for a moment. "Can I stay here?"

"Yeah, sure," the young doctor said. "I can't let you in with her while she's in intensive care, but you're welcome to be here as much as you want. If you need anything, just ask one of the nurses. They have instructions to page me anytime there's any change in her condition."

"Thanks, doctor," Brian said.

The doctor nodded and turned to go. Brian held Barbara in his arms and tried to assure her that Lindsay would be all right.

Merrick was quiet. He waited a few minutes before Brian turned back to him. "Go on, Sergeant. Let's finish up."

Merrick nodded. "How about you, Mr. Madsen? Anyone who might be angry enough at you to come after you? Maybe someone who thought you'd be driving your wife's car?"

"I can't think of anyone," Brian said, holding Barbara close to him.

Merrick ran a hand through his hair while he considered Brian's answer. When he spoke again, there was irritation in his voice. "Look, Mr. Madsen, somebody just blew up your car. Probably tried to blow up your family. Usually that would mean that there's someone in your life who doesn't like you too much. Or someone you've really pissed off. It's a lot faster investigating this kind of a case if you can give us a starting point. Any names come to mind?"

"None," Brian said. At least technically he was telling the truth. He had no idea of the name of his own personal terrorist.

Merrick looked frustrated. "Here's my number." He thrust a card at Brian. "Call me if you think of anything." Merrick watched Brian's expression before continuing. "Anything you think of might be important. Don't omit any details. Whoever did this might not be done yet."

Brian nodded. Merrick nodded curtly to Barbara, and he and Palmer walked toward the door. Brian watched them leave, wanting to tell them about the trap he was caught in, but too afraid of where it would lead.

Chapter 13

"So what do you think?" Palmer asked Merrick as they drove away from the hospital.

"I think he knows a whole lot of shit he's not telling."

"Yeah, me too." Palmer shook his head. "So why is he keeping quiet when it may get him and his family killed?"

"That, my friend, is the sixty-four thousand-dollar question," Merrick said as he made a right turn on Hope Street and drove toward downtown. "My bet is he's afraid of something. Something is going on that's scaring the shit out of this guy."

"Like somebody has the goods on him and they're threatening to share the information. I mean, he is a politician. There's always something in the closet."

"You're learning, kid." Merrick grinned. "There's hope for you yet." He was quiet for a moment, and his expression became more serious. "The only thing is that these guys usually crack easily. This son of a bitch is saying nothing even when his family is in jeopardy. If we're guessing right on this one, whatever that somebody's got on him must be pretty fucking good."

Palmer looked at Merrick questioningly. "You got any ideas?"

Merrick looked over at Palmer and nodded. He saw the light of recognition in Palmer's eyes.

"Holy shit!" Palmer exclaimed. His eyes grew wide.

"Exactly."

Bob could feel that the ropes that bound his hands were beginning to give. He was now in a kneeling position with his weight against the doorjamb to maximize the pressure on the ropes. The still air of the closet and the intense work on the ropes soaked his brow with sweat. The darkness that surrounded him was total, and the silence had an ominous quality, like the stillness hid something terrible lying in wait.

Bob used his weight and balance as he moved. He could sense that, after a few more minutes, the bindings would give, so he worked intently, concentrating on obtaining maximum friction on the rope. He was so engulfed in his task that he didn't hear the door open. Bob could feel that just a few threads were holding the rope together. He rubbed harder and faster. He could feel that he was seconds from freedom. Suddenly everything turned to darkness. He was unconscious before he hit the floor.

Chapter 14

It was only after the intensive care charge nurse assured Barbara that she would call her with any change in the condition of Lindsay or Janet that she agreed to go home long enough to sleep for a few hours. Brian called a cab to drive them home. They rode in silence, each trapped in his or her own thoughts.

Once they arrived home, they sat down on the couch, exhausted and consumed by worry and fear. Brian could see all of it on Barbara's face, and it added the familiar guilt to the weight of his own thoughts. He put his arm around her gently. He looked into her eyes and saw the worry and the pain there. But the look of innocence needing reassurance did him in. And he knew it would all come out.

Brian knelt on the floor beside the couch and touched her cheek. "Barbara, I'm so sorry."

She looked at him and smiled. "You have no reason to be sorry. It's not your fault."

The undeserved trust that she had for Brian made him feel horrible. "It may be, Barb. I did something that allowed all this to happen. The phone calls, this afternoon, all of it."

"What? What do you mean?" she asked with her brow furrowed.

He took her hand and told her about the night of the inauguration. He could see the pain of his betrayal appearing in her eyes. He didn't stop. He told her about seeing Cathy on other occasions after the inauguration. He saw the pain in her eyes turn to anger.

"I was confused. I always loved you, Barbara. I never doubted that. But I was somehow drawn in and couldn't get out."

She stared at him silently, wounded and angry.

"I knew it had to end." He paused and took a breath. "The night I went to her place to end it was the night she died."

Her hand pulled away.

"I didn't do it," Brian said quickly. "I lost the courage to tell her good-bye. I put it off until next time, and I came home at about one o'clock. She died after I left."

She stared at him icily. "The news said she had sex before she died. You had sex with her that night, didn't you?"

He nodded. "Yes, but I went there planning to end it. I swear to you."

"And when you left her?"

"She was fine."

"You son of a bitch!" Barbara screamed. She stood up and walked to the bedroom without looking back.

Brian followed her and found her staring out the bedroom window. If there had ever been any doubt, there was none now. At that moment, he knew how much he wanted to keep her love.

He walked to within a few feet of her and stopped. "I love you, Barbara," he said weakly.

She turned and looked at him. Then she said quietly, "How do I know you didn't kill her?"

He should have been expecting the question, but Brian was shocked, maybe the delivery or perhaps the thought that she could actually believe he could kill someone. "Barb, you know I could never kill anyone, don't you?"

She was quiet again. When she spoke, it was slow and measured. "I didn't think you could go out and fuck your campaign workers either. I didn't think you could betray me and our marriage. So just what do I know that I can believe?" Tears were in her eyes.

"I didn't do it." There was silence while he waited for a response and got none. "Dammit, Barbara, I didn't do it! Why would I?"

"Why would you?" she asked angrily. "Like I'm supposed to have any idea of what motivates you now? How do I know, Brian? Maybe she was threatening to tell someone. Maybe you needed to keep her from hurting your precious political career. All I know is that you're asking me to believe what you say right after confessing that our whole marriage is a lie. Why should I believe you?"

He was quiet for a moment, understanding her feelings. There was no good reason for her to believe him. He finally said softly, "Because I need you to, Barbara. Because no one else will believe me."

She stared at him with cold eyes. "Okay. I'll believe you for all the years we've been together. Or just because I want to." She hesitated. "But that doesn't mean I'll forgive you."

He nodded, moving toward her. "I know you may not. And if you do, I know it will take time. I'll do whatever it takes, Barbara." Brian leaned over to kiss her on the cheek, but she pulled away.

"How soon did she die after you left?" she asked.

"The papers say they fixed the time of her death at one thirty or two o'clock."

"Only a half hour to an hour after you left?"

He nodded. "I was the last one to see her alive, but no one knows it." He paused. "My fingerprints are all over the place."

She shot him another look of anger.

"The caller says he has the murder weapon and it has my prints on it too."

"Oh my God. The police need to know all this."

Brian shook his head emphatically. "I'm the only suspect. And he's got all the evidence." He took a deep breath. "You know that jewelry box the police just received?"

She nodded.

"That lunatic sent it to them just to let me know that he can have me picked up anytime. I had touched it. He wiped it clean before he sent it in, but he let me think—-" Brian stopped mid-sentence.

"Can't we just tell them all of this?"

Brian shook his head. "I'm still the only suspect. And I told the police that I never saw her socially. Now I'm a liar too."

She glared at him and then said in a monotone voice, "Yes, you are." She took a deep breath. "So what do we do?"

"We? You're still with me?" Brian asked tentatively.

"It means you're in trouble and I'll help you. I don't know beyond that."

He nodded. "I know I can't ask for anything more. Thank you."

She sat down on the bed. "So what do we do?"

There was a silence before he spoke. "I've started thinking about doing what he wants."

"About killing someone?" Barbara asked in a disbelieving tone.

"It's about more than whether I get charged with Cathy's murder. Think about what happened today, Barbara. He almost killed you. Even now, we don't know how Lindsay's going to do. There's just no limit to what this son of a bitch will do."

It was almost seven o'clock as Sheila stood at the door of Michael's office. "Goodnight, Michael." She waved a hand in his direction.

He looked up from a file. "Goodnight, Sheila."

She glanced at her watch. "You better leave too. Your flight takes off in just over an hour."

"Yeah, I know. Just a couple more calls and I'm out of here."

She nodded. "Have a good trip."

"I will. I'll probably come in tomorrow night when I get back. Can you have the Wellington Pharmaceutical detail ready for me by then? Let's say six o'clock?"

"No sweat. It'll be ready. Give my regards to Bob Nicholas and the San Francisco bunch, will you?"

"I will." He grinned. "You know they love you."

She smiled and then turned to go. Michael waited and listened while her footsteps faded. He gave Sheila enough time to get to the elevator before he picked up the phone.

Brian sat down on the bed next to Barbara. He struggled to find words to get past her pained expression. There was so much he wanted to say. The telephone rang, the sound startling Brian, even though the call was expected. Brian glanced at his watch. It was a little after seven o'clock. He and Barbara looked at the phone and then at each other until it rang three times.

Brian finally picked it up. "Hello?"

"Hello, Brian," the icy voice of the killer said. "I knew you wouldn't have much time to think about my offer today, having your own tragedy to deal with and everything, so I'm extending your deadline until tomorrow. Tomorrow you get to protect your family as well as yourself."

"You son of a bitch, you almost killed them," Brian shouted, seething with anger.

There was a momentary silence. Then the killer said, "Relax, Brian. It was a message. I don't aim and miss. I just wanted to show you what might happen. Understand?"

Brian said softly, "I understand."

"It all comes down to tomorrow. There won't be any more lessons." The line went dead.

Brian stared at the phone.

"What did he say?" Barbara asked.

"More of the same." He took her hand in his. "I want you to leave town for a while. Maybe for a few weeks."

She was watching his eyes. Her look was disapproving.

"Just listen," Brian said. "You need to be away from here. I can't deal with knowing this guy may come after you again."

"I'm supposed to leave you here to deal with this?"

He touched her cheek lovingly. "I'm scared shitless of this guy. There's nothing he won't do, so I need to know you're safe. There's just no choice."

She nodded reluctantly. "I could go see one of my college buddies for a week or so. Maybe Marilyn in Scottsdale."

Brian shook his head. "No. Nowhere with people who know you. There can't be any way to find you. Maybe Boise or Topeka. Somewhere you've never been and have no compelling reason to go."

"I want to stay," Barbara said with pain in her voice.

"Thank you, Barb. Really. But this guy will hurt you to get to me. Just give me two weeks. Then I'll come and get you."

She hugged Brian, and they held on to each other as if to never let go.

* * *

Sheila never quite made it to the elevator before realizing she had left her keys at her desk. She walked away from the elevator bank in the direction of the executive corridors. The click of her heels on the wood paneling broke the silence until she reached the carpeting of the hallways and her sounds disappeared. At this rate, she would get home just in time to return with morning rush hour, she told herself, letting out a deep sigh. She ran a hand through her long red hair. Her slightly turned-up nose and full lips gave her a voluptuous appeal. Her broad bedroom eyes seemed to conflict with aristocratic distance of her features. As she reached her desk, impatience was conveyed on her frown and furrowed brow.

She looked around, moved her in box slightly, and found the keys sitting on the corner of her desk. As she picked them up, she could hear Michael through the open door with an unfamiliar tone in his voice. She walked over to the wall next to the door, staying out of view, and listened. Involuntarily, she put a hand to her mouth in shock. There had to be some explanation for what she was hearing. She stood frozen in disbelief.

Moments later, the conversation abruptly ended, and Sheila heard Michael put down the phone. She walked quickly out of the office, hearing his footsteps behind her. She walked into the hallway and then ducked into the supply room, closing the door behind her. The room was the size of a walk-in closet and very dark. She left the light off and waited.

It took about five minutes for Michael to gather his materials, slip on his coat, and disappear down the corridor toward the elevators. Sheila waited in the dark of the supply room for another five minutes after hearing his footsteps before stepping out into the hallway. She looked down the hall to make sure he wasn't coming back and then walked back into his office. She moved quickly to the phone and pressed two buttons. She heard the last number that had been dialed replayed at high speed. Then it rang.

"Hello?" a male voice answered.

Sheila wasn't sure what to say. "Did you just receive a call from a man?" she finally asked.

"Yes, we did," he said in a surprised, almost desperate tone. "Do you know who it was?"

She was quiet, evaluating the situation. *What did it all mean?*

"Please tell us. We need to know who it was. He's threatening us," the man pleaded.

Sheila felt a sudden fear. *What am I doing? What would I be doing to Michael?*

"Please, who is this?" the man repeated.

The fear became too much. A sensation of panic overtook Sheila, and she put down the phone. She stood there feeling sick and then impulsively picked up the phone and dialed the police. It rang once. She returned the handset quickly to the cradle. *What would I tell them? What did I really know?*

Then she suddenly realized what she had done. Sheila had lost the connection to whomever Michael had been talking to. She had no number and no name. She stared out the office window into the darkness, unable to believe what she had heard and not knowing what to do.

* * *

Within a few hours after Barbara's reluctant agreement to leave while Brian dealt with the killer, Brian backed the rented car out of the garage. He had completed his preparation in less than two hours. It was like the script of a B movie. He had even rented the car under an assumed name, using nothing but a fictitious business card and cash.

Barbara's suitcases were in the trunk. An Auto Club pouch containing maps of four states sat on the passenger's seat. Brian turned off the ignition and climbed out of the car. He walked to the open front door and heard the phone ringing. Barbara stood by the door, staring at the telephone as if it might explode.

He walked slowly toward the telephone, knowing who was there. "Hello?"

"Don't send away your wife," the familiar voice said.

"What?"

"Don't even think about it. It won't work."

"You son of a bitch! Where the fuck are you?" Brian screamed.

"Think of your friend, Bob. You sent him out alone. Don't do the same to your wife."

Brian threw down the telephone and ran out the front door. He stood on the sidewalk and looked around. A couple kids sat on the curb a few houses away. He saw nothing else. In the other direction, there was nothing at all. He looked through the front windows of the surrounding houses. *Was the killer there, watching everything they did? Was he watching me right now?* Brian could see nothing. He jumped as Barbara touched his arm.

"What is it?" she asked gently.

"That son of a bitch is watching. He knows what we're doing and when we're doing it."

"What?" She rubbed the outside of the arm in the sling with her good hand, as if she were chilled.

"He said, 'Don't let your wife leave.' He reminded me of what happened when I sent Bob to track him."

"My God, Brian." Barbara looked at him and waited. "What do we do?"

"Maybe I tell the police everything I know and hope I'm believed and you go to Canada."

She shook her head. "I don't think I can live like that."

He nodded his understanding. There was a long silence as he reflected. "Or I could do it."

"Kill this stranger?" she asked incredulously.

"What's the alternative? Someone killing you?" He paused for a moment and then grimaced. "I called Bob's house today. Then I called everybody I know who knows him. No one's seen him. If I don't do this, I think he's dead, and maybe you are, too. I'm convinced there's nothing this guy won't do to get what he wants. The amoral live without constraint."

She was silent, so he continued, "You can be my alibi. If anyone asks, I'll have been with you watching videos. But probably no one will. I don't even know this guy, so there's not much short of what I leave behind that could tie me to his death."

Barbara looked shocked as she said, "You're seriously thinking about doing this, aren't you?"

"Maybe I have no choice. Just like he wants it."

"Bob could already be dead."

"I know. I've been thinking about that. But if he's not, I don't want to be responsible for his death too."

"What if you don't do it?"

"Then I go to the police and tell them everything. Then I wait to get arrested, and you take cover."

"I'll make some coffee," Barbara said. "It may be a long night."

Brian followed her to the kitchen and watched her put a filter in the basket. "Thanks, Barbara," he said after a moment.

"For what?" she asked without turning toward him.

"For listening. For talking this through. For not leaving." He walked to her and touched her cheek. "Whatever happens to you and me, thanks for being here now. I've been going crazy thinking about all this alone."

8She nodded. "Let's go over our choices again. Maybe there's something else we can try."

They covered every alternative, every nuance of every plan either could construct, as they sat in the living room drinking coffee. It never came out much different. Run, hide, and go to the police or go through with the murder.

It was four in the morning when Barbara fell asleep on the couch. Even the three cups of coffee she had consumed since midnight couldn't keep her awake any longer. Brian put a blanket over her and kissed her cheek. Then he went into the kitchen and made a fresh pot of coffee. He stared out the kitchen window at the dark clumps that were trees and bushes in the daylight, turning the situation over in his mind. It was getting harder to focus. He sat at the kitchen table with his head in his hands. Within a few minutes, he fell asleep.

He drifted into a dream and saw her face. He was at the same kitchen table looking out on a beautiful spring morning. Cathy stood outside the window. She looked in and saw him with that instant recognition and warm smile. She waved to him and then walked closer, reaching out and pressing her hand against the outside of the glass. Then the glass was in her hand, and she was bleeding. Her body was suddenly bruised and still, like the images broadcast after the murder.

Brian stood up and ran to her. As he reached the window, the image was suddenly Barbara's, reaching out to him with tears in her eyes. He reached out to touch her, and she pulled away. Brian awoke with a start. He looked around the kitchen and felt the pain in his heart. It was just after six in the morning, and he had made his final decision.

Chapter 15

Through a veil of sleep-induced fog, Barbara heard the doorbell ringing. She looked around the room, feeling disoriented, and then remembered her all-night discussion with Brian and realized that she must have fallen asleep on the couch. She heard the muffled and distant sound of water running, which told her Brian was in the shower. She straightened her clothing and pushed back her hair, all as reflex, knowing it would make little difference in the way she looked.

She called out, "Just a minute," as she walked toward the door. She opened the door to find familiar, though not particularly welcome, faces. "Sergeant Merit, right?" she said politely.

"Merrick, ma'am. And you remember Officer Palmer?"

The uniformed man gave a brief nod.

"Yes, I remember. How can I help you, gentlemen?"

"We need a few words with your husband, Mrs. Madsen. Is he around?"

"Well, he's in the shower at the moment."

Merrick nodded. "Fine, we'll wait."

"Come into the living room and have a seat." She gave them the direction with the wave of her hand. "I'll let him know you're here."

"Thank you, ma'am," Merrick said.

Barbara turned to go upstairs and then hesitated. "Would you like some coffee?"

Merrick almost smiled. "I was hoping you'd ask."

"And you, Officer?" She looked at the ever-silent Palmer.

He nodded, keeping his record for silence intact. He looked at her in a way that made her feel self-conscious, as if he were studying her.

"Please excuse my appearance. I fell asleep on the couch watching a movie last night, and I just woke up when the doorbell rang."

"You look fine, ma'am," Merrick said, sounding sincere.

Barbara gave him a half smile. He was a liar, but he was polite. "How do you take your coffee?" she asked in Merrick's direction.

"Just black, ma'am."

"And you, Officer?"

"Same, thanks," said Palmer.

Barbara nodded and then turned and walked from the room.

After Barbara left the room, Palmer looked over at Merrick. "You think the guy's going out the backdoor while we stand here waiting for caffeine?" He looked around the room, the way people always do when left alone for the first time in someone else's house, looking for something in the decor that would provide insight about the host. Or the way cops do when they're looking for evidence of something.

Merrick shook his head. "Not a chance. He's a politician. I'm sure he'll be quite diplomatic."

Palmer wrinkled his brow to convey his skepticism. "Yeah, right. Watch me pull a rabbit out of my hat."

Brian walked into the kitchen, buttoning his shirt. "Where are they?" he asked Barbara as she finished pouring two cups of coffee.

"In the den." She gave him a look of concern. "Don't worry," he said reassuringly. "I can handle it." He glanced at the cups. "I'll take our guests their coffee."

Barbara nodded slowly as he picked up the cups. "Be careful," she said with concern as he left the kitchen.

Brian walked into the den, and both men stood.

"Good morning, officers," he said cordially.

As always, Merrick was the one to speak. "Good morning, Mr. Madsen."

Brian handed each a cup, and the officers took a sip of the coffee. Merrick looked at the cup and nodded approvingly.

"Please sit down and be comfortable." Brian motioned to the seats they had vacated. He selected a chair across the coffee table from Merrick and to the left of Palmer. "So what gives rise to this early morning visit?" Brian asked.

"Well, sir, we're very concerned about the attack at the video store."

"It concerns me too, Sergeant. Somebody almost blew up my family."

"That's just it, Mr. Madsen. It wasn't just close to your family. It was aimed at your family. The bomb was put in your car."

"Yes, sir. I've been told that."

"So it seems clear that someone was after you or your family. Or maybe after your family to get to you."

Brian nodded and waited.

"First it was Ms. Jenkins. Now someone seems to be after you," Merrick said.

"What do you make of it?" Brian asked, fishing for information.

"Little bit too much of a coincidence for me, Mr. Madsen. What are the odds of two people who have paths that cross being under attack from two different and unrelated sources in such a short period of time?" Merrick didn't wait for any attempted response to his rhetorical question. "Pretty remote."

"Go on," Brian said, anxious to see where all this was leading.

"I'm thinking there has to be some connection," Merrick said.

"Meaning?"

"I'm not sure yet." Merrick scratched his chin, and Brian felt a sense of relief that the big build-up stopped where it did.

Merrick furrowed his brow. "Maybe a disgruntled employee. Someone with an ax to grind."

Brian nodded.

Merrick leaned forward in his seat. "Now you said you never saw Ms. Jenkins socially, didn't you, sir?"

Brian felt his pulse race. "Yes, I did." He tried not to show any reaction to the question.

"Then the common ground might be where you worked together. That would be in your election campaign, right?"

"Right."

Merrick nodded thoughtfully. "And we've looked at that. We just haven't found much there." He paused. He seemed to be watching Brian closely when he spoke again. "Can you think of anything else you and Ms. Jenkins had in common? Maybe places you went or things you did?"

Merrick had a way of honing in on sensitive areas that made Brian blanch inwardly. Once again Brian found himself wondering if Merrick knew something he wasn't letting on.

"Not that I can think of, Sergeant."

"Anyone at campaign headquarters who had an ax to grind with you or Ms. Jenkins?" Merrick asked.

"Not that I know of."

"Anyone you had to let go? Anyone who got into some kind of trouble for something they did? Anyone with a reason to be upset with the campaign or you?"

"I can't think of anyone."

"You see, Mr. Madsen, that's the real troubling thing," Merrick said, frowning.

"What's that?" Brian asked almost inaudibly.

"Well, we've been looking at Ms. Jenkins' life rather closely, as you can well imagine." He paused for effect. "Can't find anyone out there who had any dislike for her. Seems that the same is true for you, right?" He didn't wait for an answer. "Yet someone killed her, and now there's someone after you and your family. Doesn't make sense, does it?"

"I agree," Brian said. "And?"

"And we thought you might be able to shed a little light now that you've had time to reflect on things."

Brian shook his head. "I can't think of anything I haven't already said. What about the bomb? Won't that tell you something about who's doing this?"

"Maybe," Merrick said. "The lab is working on it, but we won't have results for a couple of days." Merrick stood up suddenly. "Thanks for your time and the coffee." He raised his cup and then set it down on the coffee table.

"Our pleasure, Sergeant," Brian said.

The officers walked toward the front door. Brian followed to show them out. As he opened the door, Merrick turned back to Brian. "One more question, Mr. Madsen. Have you been getting any unusual phone calls lately?"

Brian tried not to wince openly. He hesitated, maybe too long. "No, sir. Why?"

"Just a thought. Sometimes an attacker makes contact with the intended victim."

Brian nodded. His throat was constricting and preventing the passage of words.

"Let us know if anything like that happens, will you?" Merrick said.

"We will," Brian said, forcing out the words.

The officers left, and Brian closed the door behind them. Then he leaned against it. He was shaking, feeling like his legs might give out under the weight of the lies he kept telling.

Brian made his way to the bedroom. He didn't see Barbara, but he heard the shower running. He walked to the dresser and opened the bottom drawer. The gun was still wrapped in the weathered and water-stained paper. He opened the paper and took out the handgun, leaving the crumpled paper in the drawer. Taped to the gun was a folded piece of paper Brian hadn't seen before. He tore the note from the gun and unfolded it. The message was typed. It read, "6'2", one ninety-five. Closely cropped brown hair and a mustache, graying. Car is a late-model Lexus 400, dark green."

That was it. There were no names and no license plate numbers. Brian held the gun in his palm. He examined it closely. It was small, black, and absent any identifying features. He flipped open the chamber and looked inside. It was loaded. He closed the chamber and placed the gun in his briefcase. Now he was ready. He could almost feel himself beginning to sweat.

Chapter 16

Brian left his unopened briefcase on the worktable in the corner of his office. Whenever he looked in the direction of the case, the grim reminder of its contents quickened his pulse. He could think of little else. Nothing in the office could hold his attention for more than a few seconds. Every time his thoughts returned to the gun, the emotional upheaval seemed to worsen. The only reason to be in the office was to maintain some semblance of normalcy in his life before he went to do what had to be done. He couldn't help wondering if the others in the office could sense that something was wrong. The veneer seemed to wear thinner as the day wore on and Brian drew closer to the event.

Brian had left the house without telling Barbara of his decision or that he had even taken the gun. There was no point in both of them facing the horrendous expectation that lay only a few hours ahead. He would spare her what he could.

At six o'clock, Brian called Barbara. She answered on the first ring.

"Hi, Barb. It's me."

"Brian, I'm so sorry I fell asleep last night. How are you doing?"

"I'm okay. Listen, you and I are going to watch a video tonight." He allowed time for the message to penetrate.

"Oh my." Brian could hear the concern in her voice. "Are you sure?"

"Yes, I think so."

"Are you really sure, Brian?"

"No, but I have no choice. I love you, Barbara."

"I love you too. In a way, I feel like you've come back to me."

"I know. Me too. I'll see you soon."

"Take care, Brian. Hurry home."

Brian slowly returned the phone to its cradle. All that was happening had a dreamlike quality to it. Brian felt as if he were watching his life from a distance and without control. It was a sense he had felt since the nightmare morning he first learned about Cathy's murder.

Brian took a look around the office, as if viewing his surroundings for the last time. He told himself that, whatever happened, there was no turning back.

* * *

Bob had no idea how long he had been out. He knew only that his head hurt like hell and another rope was in place around his wrists. Slowly he felt around the interior of the closet. He felt hanging clothes. A couple of cardboard boxes were in one corner, but they were weak and gave way the moment he applied the force of the ropes. He made his way to the back of the closet, where he found a long, flat piece of metal that he could only guess was a ruler or yardstick of some kind. He pinned the metal between himself and the wall and began to work his ropes against it.

In less than an hour, the rope had weakened to the point where its last strands broke and Bob's arms were free. He removed the blindfold and the ropes that bound his legs. He listened carefully at the door for a full five minutes. Deciding that his captor was not there and that he had better move before that changed, he threw his shoulder into the locked door and waited for a reaction.

There was no response, so he slammed into the door again and then waited. Nothing happened, so he struck repeatedly at the door until it finally gave after ten minutes. He fell on top of the door, his now-tender shoulder the point of impact. He grimaced as a shooting pain exploded in the shoulder and down the arm. He held the injured right shoulder with his left hand and quickly glanced around him. He was alone.

Bob moved around cautiously and quickly determined that he was all alone in a small cabin. There was a small living room with an oversized couch and chair, unused in some time as they were both covered with sheets, which in turn were covered with dust. There was a potbellied fireplace and a small window, through which only a wooded area comprised of tall pines was visible. He noted that there were no paintings, pictures, or personal touches of any kind in the room.

Bob walked from the small living room into an even smaller kitchen, consisting of a dated yellow countertop with inlaid sink, a few scattered cupboards, and a half-size refrigerator. He opened the refrigerator door and found it empty. He opened the cupboards and found a few old, stained glasses and mugs. There was no sign of occupancy or recent use.

Bob moved from the kitchen into a small bedroom. He saw a double bed without linen and a nightstand. The room was otherwise empty. From there, he moved slowly into the bathroom. A toilet, sink, and a small shower were the only items in the room. The medicine cabinet was empty—no toothbrush, shampoo, or shaving equipment. Bob knew it was no coincidence that there were no trails for him to follow in identifying who had abducted him. He rubbed at his sore arm and wondered how long he had been here. He had no idea.

Until he peered out through the living room window, he hadn't even known whether it was day or night. He made his way to the bedroom window and looked out at the front of the cabin. There were no cars. He could see nothing but a flat patch of dirt leading into woods less than twenty feet away.

Bob slowly made his way out the front door. He had been left alone. Out front, he could see that the cabin was well isolated, a lake on one side and woods on the other three. He saw no neighbors. He walked around the side of the cabin and found tire tracks that led through the woods and the makeshift road that led away from the cabin. The road was his best chance of reconnecting with civilization.

Bob began to jog in the rut made by a heavily treaded tire. It took him into woods that blocked the sun and made it appear as if twilight had arrived. After about fifteen minutes, he jogged out of the woods and into a clearing. The tire tracks became a real dirt road. He followed it for five minutes and then saw another cabin, a bigger one, in the distance. As he drew closer, Bob could make out cars around the structure. It was a general store. He stopped and put his hands on his knees, trying to regain his breath. Every part of his body ached, but that was just soreness. The pain in his head was excruciating.

A phone was outside the store. Bob ran inside and saw a willowy, gray-haired man of about sixty behind the counter, talking to a rotund woman who appeared to be in her late thirties.

Bob looked from one to the other and then spoke to both. "Where am I?" he asked loudly.

"What?" the man asked incredulously.

"Where is this place? I need to know where we are." A desperate quality was in his tone.

The large woman regarded disheveled clothing and bruised body as she might a visitor from outer space. "Toner Highway at Route Thirty," the man behind the counter shouted.

"Thanks," Bob said and ran out the front door and back to the phone. He called 9-1-1 and immediately got through.

"9-1-1 emergency," a woman's placid voice said.

"I need help," Bob said, taking a moment to catch his breath.

"What is it, sir?" the woman said evenly.

"I've been kidnapped, tied up, and held captive in a closet. I just managed to escape." Bob said, doing his best to keep calm.

"What is your name, sir?" the woman asked.

"Galvin. Robert Galvin."

"I have you at Toner Highway, Palmer Lake. Can you verify?"

"I'm told it's Toner Highway and Route Thirty," Bob said anxiously, glancing toward the dirt road he had taken from the woods to make sure he hadn't been followed.

"Okay, sir, you relax. We'll have a car at your location within ten minutes."

"Thank you." Bob then took a deep breath as he put down the phone.

Immense relief swept over him with the knowledge that he had made good his escape and the police were on the way. He turned to make his way back to one of the seats inside the store, where he could catch his breath as he waited. As he turned, he saw the speeding car coming directly at him. It was within fifteen feet. Bob dove with all the strength left in him. He was flying through the air and then on the hood of the vehicle, rolling into the blackness as he lost consciousness.

Chapter 17

At six thirty, Brian drove past 600 Fifth Street. It was one more in a series of ground floor banks with thirty-five floors of offices stacked above. Brian circled the block, studying the building and the driveways leading in and out. He thought about how long it would take to get out of the parking structure and the neighborhood itself. After driving past the building a second time, he drove back toward Ninth Street. When he reached Ninth, he made a right and drove precisely two miles, slowing to take note of his surroundings. An old man in tattered clothing, pushing a shopping cart full of cardboard, cloth, and aluminum cans, walked slowly along the sidewalk. The surrounding buildings had been boarded up, or simply left with broken windows and now served as shelter for the locals. Makeshift fences and barricades had fallen down or been torn down. Trash covered the landscape. Groups of teens and preteens traveled in packs of four or more. It would be here that Brian left the wallet and credit cards for consumption by the unfortunate soul who, for a brief period, would think it was his lucky day.

Comfortable with the route, Brian drove back to Fifth Street, stopping at a coffee shop three blocks from his destination. It took fifteen minutes to find a metered parking space on the street. He wanted to be sure that no parking lot records would contain an entry bearing his license plate number. Brian put several coins into the meter, saw that it yielded an hour, and went into the coffee shop. There was a red counter fronted by several round backless stools. Only two of the stools were occupied, one by an elderly man with unkempt, greasy hair and a full gray beard and the other by a man in a business suit, sipping a cup of coffee and reading the *Wall Street Journal*. Neither of them looked in Brian's direction as he entered.

Brian sat in one of several small booths that bordered the window. He ordered a hamburger and a cup of coffee from a bored-looking server in her late twenties, who stared out the window while she waited for his order. She scribbled the order briefly on a notepad and then walked away without a word.

When the hamburger arrived, it was just before seven. *Plenty of time.* His stomach was churning, and he wondered why he had ordered anything to eat. Just looking at the food made him feel queasy. An unshakable feeling of doom was also in the air. He was moving toward the moment when he would do something he never thought himself capable of, when he would end a man's life and forever change his own. He held up his hand and watched it visibly shaking. He knew he had to find some measure of control just to make it through the night that lay ahead.

At seven thirty, Brian finished his second cup of coffee. He left the hamburger untouched. He put seven dollars on the table and walked to the door without making eye contact with the customers or the server, none of whom paid him the slightest bit of attention.

Brian moved the car to another metered space a block away from the office building. Many cars were now gone, and it was easier to find a parking space. It took just over a minute to walk casually to the building. Brian planned to return at that same slow pace, so as to avoid attracting attention.

Arriving at the building, Brian found the three stairways that led down to the underground parking garage. He took the first stairway down to level number five and then looked for the green Lexus. He found two of them on opposite ends of the lot. One was parked near stairwell number one; the other was by stairwell number three. Brian walked each of the stairwells from the fifth level to the street, noting how long it took and where he emerged in relation to where he had parked. Then he returned to level number five, just in time to see a tall blonde woman climbing into the Lexus parked adjacent to stairwell number one. His man was parked by stairwell three. Brian checked his watch. It was seven forty-eight. It was too early for Ross to be leaving.

Brian looked around and found a narrow walkway, formed by the structure wall and a large column, just a few feet from the Lexus. He walked over and leaned behind the column. From there he could watch the car and emerge from the shadows when the time was right. The garage was cool, but Brian was sweating. He told himself to relax. He checked his watch again. It was seven fifty-three.

* * *

Barbara sat in the den, thinking about Brian and nervously checking the time. Seven fifty-three. Her eyes frequently traveled between the telephone and her watch. The silence was unbearable, and time dragged. When the doorbell rang, the sudden intrusion into her solitude made her let out a scream. She put a hand to her heart.

"Shit," she said, working to slow her pulse.

As she walked to the door, Barbara wondered who would possibly be showing up now. She was preoccupied and didn't need to entertain tonight.

When she opened the door, Sergeant Merrick nodded to her. "Good evening, ma'am."

Palmer silently removed his hat and gave a nod.

"May we speak with your husband for a few minutes?" Merrick asked.

"I'm sorry. He's not home at the moment."

"Really?" Merrick asked with a raised eyebrow. "And where would he be?"

Barbara scowled. "He had a business meeting tonight. Not that there's any reason I should have to tell you where he is."

"I didn't mean to upset you, Mrs. Madsen, but we need to talk to him. Do you know where his meeting is?"

"No, not specifically."

They regarded her with curiosity.

"The meeting is over on the west side somewhere. I know that," Barbara said with a sigh.

"When do you expect him home?"

"I'm sorry. I'm not sure." She thought about how this conversation subverted their plan to say she and Brian had been at home watching videos. She had no way of getting word to him.

Merrick nodded. "Please tell him we stopped by, will you?"

"I will," Barbara said.

Merrick gave her a nod, and the men turned and walked toward their car. Barbara watched for a moment and then closed the door, wishing she had some way to communicate with Brian.

Chapter 18

Walking down the path toward the street, Merrick and Palmer heard Barbara close the door behind them.

As they approached the car, Palmer was the first to speak. "Is she lying, or doesn't she know where he is?"

"Not sure," Merrick said. "Even if she's lying about where he is, could be she just doesn't think it's our business. She got pretty indignant."

"Could be." Palmer paused and then said, "Maybe we should have told her where he is right now to watch the reaction. Then maybe she could tell us what he's up to."

Merrick shook his head. "No, we'll wait until we get a report about what he does from here. Then we'll see if he lies about where he was."

"You really think this guy killed her?"

"I don't know," said Merrick. "We know he's lying about how well he knew her, but that could be just because he doesn't want the missus to know he was screwing around."

Palmer nodded.

"We'll watch him some more, and maybe he'll show us," Merrick said.

"I think the son of a bitch did it," Palmer said as he climbed behind the wheel of the car.

Merrick slid into the passenger seat, and the car moved away from the curb. "This is Merrick. Patch me through to Bellows," he said into the car radio.

"One second, Sergeant."

The line crackled for several seconds. Then a deep voice came on the line.

"This is Bellows."

"What's he up to?" Merrick asked.

"We don't have him in sight at the moment, Sergeant."

"What the fuck happened?" Merrick asked incredulously. "You lost him?"

"Just temporarily, Sergeant. We'll find him again."

Merrick waited for an explanation, suppressing his anger.

"We followed him to a coffee shop downtown. He came out twenty minutes ago and started driving around town. We lost him a few minutes ago, but he couldn't have gone far. We've got units watching the freeway ramps and major arteries out of the downtown area. We know he's still right around here."

"That's fucking great." Then Merrick drew a breath and took a moment to calm himself before continuing. "At this point we have to assume that he was he onto you, so approach cautiously."

"We'll find him," Bellows said with confidence Merrick didn't share.

"Get help if you need it, but find him. Then call me back." Merrick picked up the phone and looked at Palmer. "Those guys could fuck up a wet dream."

Palmer nodded and then accelerated toward downtown.

Chapter 19

It was eight ten when a man emerged from the parking structure elevator. The footfalls grew louder as he approached and moved into the light, giving Brian a view of his features. Brian watched him move directly toward the green Lexus, now the only car in the area. There was no doubt: six foot two, close-cropped brown hair, and mustache. It was him, the man Brian was to kill without ever knowing.

Brian stepped quietly out of the shadows and raised the gun. He was within fifteen feet from Jason Ross and slightly to the right of the spot he would cross as he walked straight for the car. His attention was cast toward the car and then to the ground in front of him. Brian pointed the gun directly at him. He held it with both hands, trying unsuccessfully to keep it steady.

The gun shook, betraying his nervousness. "Hold it," Brian heard himself saying.

The voice caught Jason by surprise. He looked over at Brian with wide eyes, stopped in his tracks, and raised his hands.

"Don't move," Brian said, moving to close the distance between them. He wasn't sure why he was moving in so close, whether it was to get a better look at the man, to delay the decision, or just to be sure he wouldn't miss.

"All right. Just don't shoot," Jason said with his hands still in the air. "You can have anything you want. My wallet, car keys, anything you want. Just don't shoot."

Brian walked closer, stopping five feet from him. For a moment, the men stood staring at one another with neither moving. Brian had reached that point through survival instinct, and Jason was operating on that same instinct now. Brian felt the sweat on his brow as he wondered whether he could go any further when he heard the squeal of tires somewhere behind him. He glanced over his shoulder toward the voice.

As Brian realized that the structure's acoustics had created the illusion that the distant sound was close behind him, Jason acted in desperation, striking out at Brian with his hand.

Brian saw the punch coming and jumped back. The blow grazed his shoulder. Brian jabbed into Jason's midsection in an attempt to regain control. Jason doubled over, momentarily subdued, and then suddenly threw himself at Brian. The two hit the cement floor of the garage, and the gun flew from Brian's hand. They wrestled until Brian was pushed backward into a vertical column and fell to the ground.

Jason then he ran toward Brian, who was halfway between the ground and a standing position. As Jason came at him, Brian saw the gun three feet away and dove for it. Jason saw it too and attempted to kick it away. Jason's kick hit Brian's hand as he grabbed for the gun. Brian felt a sudden surge of pain but held on. He lay on the ground, pointing the weapon at Jason. Brian was no longer shaking. For the first time, he held the gun still.

Five floors above, Bellows drove his police cruiser into the parking garage. He began to search the sparsely populated structure, level by level, for any sign of Brian. The building-by-building search was taking too damn long. Bellows was cursing himself for letting Brian disappear, seemingly into thin air. He also knew that Merrick was going to have his ass for this screwup.

Jason had no fight left in him. His hands stayed up, and he stood still, breathing heavily. He seemed resigned to whatever would come next. Brian looked into Jason's eyes and saw the depth of his fear. It was then that Brian knew he would not kill Jason. There was only one man that he would kill if they could meet him face-to-face, and that man would never face him.

Brian held the gun on Jason as he said, "I don't want to kill you." He paused to breathe, still recovering from the exertion of the struggle. "I don't even know you."

Jason nodded. "I'll give you anything you want," he was pleading. "Please don't shoot me."

Brian said softly, "I don't want your money."

"What do you want?" Gasps punctuated the question as Jason bent slightly forward and held his stomach, trying to regain normal breathing. The look on his face conveyed a combination of fear and bewilderment.

Brian had a hard time putting what he needed to say into words that made any sense. "I don't want anything of yours. I just need to talk to you."

"You want to talk?" Jason asked incredulously. "With a gun in a parking garage?"

Brian allowed his arm to fall and the gun to rest at his side. "Is there a place we can talk?"

"Two minutes ago, you were going to shoot me. Now, I'm supposed to invite you up for a chat? Shall I make some coffee?"

"This is about your safety as well as mine," Brian said. "You have a much bigger threat than me to worry about."

Jason studied Brian's desperate expression closely, assessing. He hesitated and then nodded. "Let's go back to my office."

The two walked toward the elevator with Brian still holding the gun at his side. The black-and-white drove onto level five of the structure. Bellows scoured the area in search of Brian. There was no sign. He ran a hand through his brown crew cut and shook his head. His round cheeks, soft features, and the wide eyes of worry made him look substantially younger than his thirty years. Looking young made weather-beaten street cops think you were a rookie even before you made a rookie mistake. He wasn't happy about the reaction this situation would get, and he wasn't looking forward to telling Merrick that Madsen still hadn't been found.

Bellows picked up the radio and patched in to the other units involved in the search. "Any sign of our man, Gifford?"

"None," a deep male voice answered. "I've done all eight structures three times. Nothing."

Bellows let out a long breath. "What is this guy, fucking Houdini?"

"Could be," Gifford said. "Neither of the units has seen anything, and I just talked to both."

"Have you spoken to Merrick?" Bellows asked.

"Not a chance. This is your assignment. You get that little pleasure."

"Yeah, I know. Just keep looking. I want this guy found." Bellows slammed down the radio and headed for level six.

* * *

Brian pushed the gun under his belt, and he and Jason walked past the guard at the entry to the building. The white-haired, uniformed man sat behind a console of monitors. He looked up from behind a magazine just long enough to lend a nod of recognition to Jason and then went back to the magazine.

They were silent during the elevator ride to the executive offices. Brian thought about the implications of not killing this man. The decision was one to endanger his own family. He thought about spending the rest of his life in jail for the murder of a woman who had loved him.

They walked into Jason's office, and he hit the light switch. Jason walked toward the large walnut desk on the far side of the room.

"No," Brian said, startling Jason. "Not over there. Stay over here." He pointed to the couch and chair against the wall near the center of the room.

Jason walked back and sat on the couch. Brian sat in the adjacent chair facing the door and looked at Jason while he considered what to say.

Brian drew a deep breath. "There's really no way to ease into this, but someone wants you dead."

Jason frowned. "Judging by what happened downstairs, I'd say that's probably you."

"No, it's not me. I don't even know you."

Jason nodded. "If you say so. But usually strangers aren't out to gun me down."

Brian rubbed his eyes before continuing, "I'm being blackmailed. Either I was to kill you or someone kills my family and I go to jail."

"So you decided to kill me because someone threatened you?"

Brian shook his head. "No, I wasn't just threatened. My wife, her sister, and her niece got out of our car just before it exploded. My wife and her sister were torn up, but our niece is still critical. The bomb was in our car to convince me I had to do what I was told."

Jason was nodding. "I remember. I saw it on the news."

Brian considered him closely. "Then you know who I am?"

"Yeah, now I do. The way we met downstairs was a little out of context. Your face was familiar, but I couldn't place you." He furrowed his brow. "Like I said, I saw you on the news. There was some speculation that whoever killed Cathy Jenkins was after you too. No one had any idea why." He grinned. "I also keep an eye on politics. Your face was on a number of posters before the election."

Brian nodded. "Did you know Cathy Jenkins?"

"Yes. We were in a number of meetings together over the years. I liked her. She knew her stuff."

Brian felt a sudden sadness for Cathy and himself. He missed her. "I sent out an investigator to find the blackmailer. He's a close friend of mine and he hasn't come back." Brian searched Jason's face for acknowledgment. His expression gave away nothing. "It's all because this bastard wants you dead."

Jason shook his head and sat forward in his chair. "That's crazy. Who would want to kill me?"

"That's what I have to find out before this psycho finds out you're still walking around and goes after my family."

"No one would want to kill me." He gave Brian a look that said he was still evaluating. "Until you, no one ever tried."

Brian ignored the comment. "Obviously somebody wants you dead enough to implicate me in a murder and go after my family. Someone will go to any lengths to get to you without leaving tracks."

Jason regarded him suspiciously, and Brian knew he had to fill in a few gaps.

"Cathy and I were involved," he said reluctantly. "We thought no one knew. Someone did." He watched Jason's face as he absorbed the information, awaiting more. "I was with Cathy the night she died. I left her at one in the morning. I went home and went to bed. When I got up in the morning, her murder was all over the news. My fingerprints were everywhere, so I sat at home waiting for the police to come and get me, still trying to conceal the relationship from my wife." He paused and drew a breath, involuntarily shaking his head, as if surprised by it all, even now.

Jason studied him intently but remained quiet, waiting for Brian to continue.

"I should have been the prime suspect, but the police never came. Instead, I got a phone call from a guy who told me he sanitized the place. All my prints are gone, except the ones on the items he took from the apartment and can deliver to the police at any time. He tells me that unless I cooperate ... " Brian's voice trailed off, and he looked down at his hands. He looked back to Jason before continuing, "Then came a series of events to convince me I had no choice, including bombing the car and almost killing my family."

Jason was shaking his head. His expression was incredulous. "Not only do I go to jail, my family dies. That's why I'm here tonight," Brian said, feeling a tear cloud his eye.

Jason nodded and then loosened his tie as he thought it through. "So are you going to do it? Are you going to kill me?"

"No. But I'm not going to let you call the police either."

Jason nodded.

"A total stranger set me up to go to jail and will kill my family to get me to kill you. So who wants you dead that bad?" Brian asked again.

"I really don't know."

"Who hates you?" Brian shouted.

Jason stared at Brian blankly. Brian figured he was assessing whether Brian was a lunatic.

Then Jason nodded and sucked in air. "In a business sense, a lot of people. I take companies. I fire people. But I don't think any one of them would be out to kill me."

"I need a list," Brian said. "I need to know who hates you the most."

Jason nodded and then was silent for a while. Brian let him think. "There's only three that come to mind."

"Who?"

"Jack Eastin is my cousin in Ohio. He's hated me forever."

"Why?"

"Because I married his fiancée two days before they were going to get married. He even threatened me a couple of times over it. But that was twelve years ago, and I haven't heard from him in the last three years."

Brian nodded. "Who else?"

"Mike Hayward. He works for the company. We've been rivals for years. Lately we've been competing for the top job around here. The CEO is about to retire. We both know that the job is going to me, but it's not public yet."

"Who's the third?"

Jason hesitated.

"Come on. I have to know," Brian said angrily.

"Connie Taylor. She and I slept together for a few years. I broke it off five or six months ago."

"Anything more to it?" Brian asked.

"A little. She thought I was going to leave my wife for her. She was angry when I told her that wasn't going to happen." Jason stood and walked over to his desk.

Brian watched him nervously, still holding the gun tightly, but said nothing. Jason pulled an address book from his desk and flipped through the pages. Then he began scribbling on a notepad. He walked back to Brian and handed him the paper.

"These are the names and phone numbers." Jason sat back down across from Brian. "I don't know if anything here will help you. I've got no fans on this list, but I don't think any of them would kill me."

Brian nodded and stood. "Are you going to have me picked up?"

Jason stood once more and looked at Brian squarely. "No, I believe what you've told me. Besides, you've got enough to worry about." He extended a hand to Brian. Brian studied him. Then they shook hands.

"Listen, whatever you find out from those on my hate list, don't publish it, all right? I'd like to keep my biggest fuck-ups as confidential as I can."

Brian nodded, smiling his understanding. Then he turned to go.

"One more thing," Jason said. "If I can help you with anything, call me."

Brian nodded. "Thanks. We both may need all the help we can get."

Chapter 20

Brian pulled into the driveway and climbed out of the car. As he walked to the front door, he scoured the neighborhood. It had become habit to search for the unseen eyes that constantly watched him. Three houses away, two teenage girls were washing an old Mustang in the driveway. They giggled as one turned the hose on the other. There was nothing out of the ordinary in any direction.

Brian walked into the house. "Barbara," he yelled out, walking into the living room.

There was no answer. He walked into the kitchen and found a note on the counter. The note said Barbara had gone to Janet's and that Brian should call and she would come right home.

Brian walked into the living room and picked up the phone. He started to dial Janet's number and then paused. He extracted Jason's hate list from his pocket and regarded the names. He would start with the one who seemed most likely, Connie Taylor.

Hell hath no fury, he thought to himself as he dialed the number.

A woman's voice answered on the third ring. "Hello."

"Connie Taylor, please."

"Speaking."

"Ms. Taylor, this is Investigator Timmons with the LAPD. I have a couple questions for you."

Nervousness was in her voice as she asked, "About what?"

"Jason Ross."

There was a slight pause. "What about him?"

"Someone tried to kill Mr. Ross tonight. I wonder what you might be able to tell me about that?" Brian wished there was a way to talk to her in person to watch her face and her demeanor.

That was the way the cops would really do it, but he didn't have official ID that would pass. He figured that he had better settle for the phone call and hope she bought it.

"Really?" she asked. The surprise sounded genuine.

"What can you tell me, Ms. Taylor?"

There was a brief silence. Then she said, "I don't have anything to say about Mr. Ross."

"Well, ma'am, you can tell me now, or I can send a car to bring you to the station, and you can tell me in person," Brian said in a tone he hoped sounded forceful.

"I can't tell you anything about tonight. I haven't seen Jason in two or three months, although I wouldn't lose a lot of sleep if someone did kill that son of a bitch."

Brian took a deep breath and then asked, "Where were you tonight, Ms. Taylor?"

"Fortunately, I was home with my boyfriend and my parents, who are here from Portland."

"You were there all evening?"

"All evening," she said without hesitation.

"Thanks, Ms. Taylor. We'll get back to you if we need to talk further." Brian slowly put down the phone.

He looked at the other two names on the list and then decided to call Barbara first to tell her that he didn't go through with it and to have her come home and be with him. He knew she would be relieved. As Brian reached for the phone, it rang.

He was startled but picked it up before the second ring. "Hello?"

"Brian," said the voice that haunted him, "you didn't do it, did you? I'm disappointed. And I'm going to have to show you that the time for talking is over."

Brian felt a sense of panic. "Look, I tried. I just couldn't do it," he said quickly.

"By tomorrow you'll wish that you had. The murder weapon is on its way, and you're no longer a free man." The line went dead.

Brian dialed Janet's house and told Barbara that he hadn't killed Jason. Then he told her about the call. She said she would be right home.

It was another night of fitful sleep. At three in the morning, Brian drifted off into one more nightmare. He was driving down the street. He looked over to see Cathy in the passenger seat smiling at him. She leaned over and kissed him on the cheek. He looked briefly at the road ahead and then turned back to see her smile. She was gone. Barbara was in the seat, looking straight ahead with a tear rolling down her face. She looked at Brian for just a second and then opened the door and leaped from the speeding car.

Brian leaped up in bed with a start. He wiped the sweat from his forehead and immediately thought of the murder weapon, whatever it was, on the way to the police. He would have only a few hours left as a free man. He thought about the bomb in the car. He thought about Bob, fearing the worst. His head felt like it had been split open with a hammer, and he knew there would be no more sleep.

Brian walked to the kitchen and stood in front of the window, watching the sun come up. It was a little before seven. He had been thinking about how to avoid arrest today when the police linked the murder weapon to him, as they inevitably would. He told himself it might not happen. But he knew better. The psychotic bastard who had been calling him was no bluffer. He had proven that already.

Brian thought about running, about packing a suitcase and heading somewhere else, anywhere else. No car, no credit cards, and no home. A new identity, odd jobs, and different names. Images of Richard Kimble came to mind. *And what about Barbara? Could I just leave her while I searched for his nameless, faceless version of the one-armed man?* He knew he couldn't do it. His only chance was the long shot. He had to identify the voice on the phone and then prove he was the killer ... and all in the next few hours. Brian wouldn't let himself give up, though he knew he might as well be trying to jump the Grand Canyon on a pogo stick.

He pulled the wrinkled list from his pocket and dialed back east. It was a decent hour in the morning there.

"Hello?" said the voice of an elderly woman.

"May I speak to Jack Eastin, please?" Brian said in a weak voice.

The woman was quiet for too long. Then she began to cry. "I'm so sorry. I have to start learning to deal with this." As she breathed heavily, she said, "Jack died in a plane crash two weeks ago. Were you a friend of his?"

Brian didn't know what to say. "Yes, we went to college together," he finally managed. "It had been a long time, so I figured I'd call and say hi."

"I know he would have liked that. I'm Edith, Jack's mother. What's your name?"

Brian made up a name. The woman said she thought Jack might have mentioned him before. She was a sweet woman, and by the end of the call, Brian had promised to stay in touch and taken down the address to send a donation in Jack's name. Brian hung up the phone, feeling sadness for the loss of a friend he had never known.

It was seven forty-five when Brian called Michael Hayward's office.

"Hello, Michael Hayward's office," a friendly female voice said.

The voice was familiar to Brian, but he couldn't place it. "Michael Hayward, please."

"I'm sorry, he's traveling today and won't be back in town until this evening. Can I take a message for him?"

Something clicked in Brian's mind. It was her, the woman who had called him right after he had hung with the killer. She had asked him about the threatening call and then hung up. Brian was almost sure, but he wanted to hear her say more. He had to keep her talking.

"Do you expect he'll be in later today?"

"I'm not sure. If he does make it in, it won't be until late afternoon or evening. Whom should I say called?"

"I'm a friend of his. I'll call back later."

Brian hung up and then leaned back in his chair and closed his eyes. He took a few moments to digest this new information and then to plan. He dialed Jason Ross' number.

"Jason Ross' office." This woman's voice was all business.

"This is Brian Madsen. May I speak with Mr. Ross, please?"

"Sorry, Mr. Madsen. He's in a meeting right now. Can I have him call you back later?"

"No. Tell him I'm on the line and that it's an emergency. He'll want to take the call."

This time there was irritation in the voice as she said, "Just a moment, sir."

Within thirty seconds, Jason was on the line. "I didn't think I'd hear from you so quickly."

"I didn't think you would either. I need to know what kind of car Michael Hayward drives. Do you know?"

"Yeah, I've seen it once or twice. It's a late-model Jaguar, one of the bigger ones."

"What color?"

"It's a burgundy color."

"Where does he park it?" Brian asked excitedly.

"He parks on the same level I do, usually several rows to the west." He paused. "You're not going to come take potshots at him in the garage, are you?"

"No more of that. I just need to be able to tell if he's around."

"Okay," Jason said reluctantly.

"I only have one more question," Brian said. "How do I get to Hayward's office? I mean, once I'm in the building?"

Jason gave him directions from the elevator and then paused. "One more thing," he said. "Have you learned about the people on that list I gave you?"

"Yes, I did. At first opportunity I'll share it with you. Right now, I've got to go."

"Good luck."

"Thanks. I need it," Brian said and hung up hurriedly.

Brian went to two electronics store before he found what he needed. Brian looked the unit over one more time and then nodded to himself. It was easy to control, and it was small enough to hide. At four o'clock, he arrived home to find the house empty. He felt a sense of disappointment that he wouldn't see Barbara before he left. Brian told himself it was for the best. He didn't want to tell her of his plan until he knew for sure.

He sat on the couch and grabbed the remote. He hit the power button, and the set roared to life with an electrical gasp. He hit the channel button until he found the news. Brian didn't have to wait long to confirm his worst fears.

A balding man with a bushy mustache stood outside the police station, speaking into a large microphone. "Police have now confirmed that a fireplace tool recovered early this morning was the murder weapon in the brutal slaying of local businesswoman Cathy Jenkins. Although not confirmed by police sources, it is believed they have a suspect in the killings based upon fingerprints and other forensic evidence taken from the tool." A picture of the fireplace poker flashed across the screen.

"We'll keep you posted as more is received on this breaking story. For now, we can only say that the police expect to have more to report within the next few hours. This is Hank Morales, reporting for NBC News."

Brian turned off the set. They now had his fingerprints. It wouldn't be long before the police swarmed the house and his office. He grabbed a coat from the hall closet and walked out the front door. There were distant sirens as he opened the car door. He knew the sirens weren't for him. There would be no warning when they came for him. It was just a grim reminder of what was to come.

Chapter 21

It was five forty when Brian arrived at the International Resources building. He parked and walked around the outside of the imposing structure. The familiar feeling of impending disaster had returned. *And why not?* he thought to himself. He was about to go to jail. He had fleeting thoughts of a pronouncement of guilt for first-degree murder. He was the last man to see Cathy alive, to sleep with her, and to be with her within the hour before her brutal death. Brian visualized the pictures of her bashed-in skull that would be passed around to a jury, the same jury that would have no trouble finding the motive, his need to cover the undisclosed affair from the constituents and his wife. He envisioned himself in chains and prison garb, being walked toward a small room where the lethal injection would be administered. He felt a pain in the pit of his stomach.

He brought his thoughts back to the present, and he spotted what he'd been looking for, an elderly man of slight build wearing a custodian's one-piece jumpsuit with International Resource embossed on the breast pocket. The man worked alone, applying polish to the expansive gray marble that decorated the lower fifteen feet of the structure. Brian stood beside the man before his presence was noticed. Then the man looked at him with a serious expression and gave a single nod of acknowledgment.

"Looks like hard work," Brian said.

"Hard enough," the old man said without slowing the circular movement of his polishing arm.

After a few moments of watching the man work, Brian tried to engage him again. "What time you work till?"

The man studied him for a moment. Then he said, "Eight o'clock. Why do you need to know?"

"Oh, I don't know. Just figured that there might be a way I can help you."

"Help me?" the man asked.

"Yeah, that's right." Brian put a finger to his lips as if to appear thoughtful. "I bet there's things you'd rather be doing."

The man nodded. "Damn straight. Most anything."

"So how about if I relieve you and you take the day off?"

The man studied him and furrowed his brow. "Is this some kind of a test? You with personnel or something?"

"No, I don't work for the company."

The man regarded Brian skeptically. "Why do you want to give me time off? Besides, you don't look like no janitor."

Brian smiled as he noticed that the name on the shirt said Willie. "Well, Willie, let's just say I'd like to do you a favor. No one will know."

The man looked down at his shirt and then back up at Brian. "My name's not Willie. It's Carl. This is just a backup shirt cuz mine's in the wash."

Brian nodded. "Okay, so what do you think, Carl?"

The man stared at him. The skepticism was as clear as ever. "I don't think so, mister. I need this job more than I need a couple of hours off."

Brian nodded. "That's fair. How about if you had the time off and a hundred dollars?"

The man's eyes flew open. "You're gonna give me a hundred dollars and finish my job for the day?"

"That's right," Brian said, grinning slightly.

"Why?"

"Because I want to try your job. I've never done it before. And like I said, I want to do you a favor."

Carl stood there transfixed, as if unsure of what he was getting into. "I don't think so. Things might go wrong."

"Nothing will go wrong, Carl. I'll do a damned good job for you." He reached into his wallet and pulled out three bills. "Three hundred dollars to have me fill in for you. You won't get a deal like that again."

Carl's eyes opened wide as he gazed at the three bills Brian fanned out in front of him. After about thirty seconds of silence, he took the money and began telling Brian where the supplies were. Brian listened, nodding periodically. His thoughts traveled to what was to come. When the man was done, Brian assured him he had it all.

"Now let me have your uniform," Brian said.

"What do you mean?"

"I mean, I need your uniform. I can't run around here doing your job dressed in a suit, can I?"

"Yeah, I know, but my uniform, man. That's awfully personal."

"Personal?" Brian pointed to the pocket inscribed with "Willie." "You're no more Willie than I am. What's so personal about a uniform with some other guy's name on it?"

The man frowned.

"Besides, I'll put it in the supply room before I leave, all right?"

After a slight hesitation, Carl nodded his assent.

Within five minutes, Brian wore the uniform and rubbed at the marble where Carl had stopped. Upon satisfying himself that Brian was doing the work, Carl waved the money and said thanks. Then he turned and moved toward the employee parking area. Brian watched until Carl disappeared from view and then moved quickly to the front door of the building.

Brian placed what he needed in the uniform breast pocket. Then he checked it to make sure the flap closed over its contents. He walked through the lobby of the building, still carrying the polishing rags. He whistled what he thought would sound to others as the unfathomable tune of the preoccupied as he walked past the guard in the direction of the supply room Carl had told him about. Through peripheral vision, he saw the guard stand and look in his direction. Brian just kept going until he saw the man sit back down, apparently satisfied that the unknown face was a new custodian. When he saw the guard turn away his attention, Brian made a right turn and headed for the main elevator bank.

To his relief, Brian rode up to the executive floor alone. As he stepped out of the elevator, he checked his watch. Six fifteen. He followed the directions to Michael Hayward's office that Jason Ross had supplied. Everything was as described. He walked down the main corridor to the "T" junction and then turned left. The suite of offices in the corner would belong to Hayward. Brian chided himself for having come this far without knowing whether Hayward was even in the building. The police would already be looking for him, and there would be no second chance.

As he entered the outer office of the suite, Brian saw an attractive woman on the telephone. He picked up his pace and walked toward her, on his way to the inner sanctum. He looked away from the woman as he approached and then walked past her toward the interior door. He still carried his polishing cloth.

The woman put down the telephone and stood. "Just a minute, please," she called after Brian. "You can't go in there. The business day isn't over."

Brian felt a sense of relief. Her concern meant that Hayward was probably inside. Brian continued walking.

The secretary came around the desk and ran toward Hayward's door. "You can't go in there yet."

Brian recognized the voice. It was the woman who had called him back after the caller had hung up. He glanced at her, wanting a better look at the face that went with the voice. She wore a long green and black skirt and a full-collared white blouse befitting the executive image. She had a slightly turned-up nose, and her full lips were fashioned into a frown. There was determination on her face.

Brian stopped. "Look, lady. I just go where they send me."

"Well, you can't go in there while Mr. Hayward is working."

"Nothing I can do, ma'am. I got my orders."

"Now you look," she said and hesitated, looking at his breast pocket, "Willie. I have my orders too. And my orders are that no one goes in without the boss's approval."

Brian shook his head. "You don't want to get me fired now, do you, ma'am?"

"You go in there, and I can almost guarantee that's what happens."

Brian nodded. "All right. I understand. Can you call my boss and say so?"

She looked wary.

"If I go back without explanation ..." Brian shrugged, leaving the likely horror to her imagination.

She nodded. "Okay, who do I call?"

"Umm, Bob Galvin in maintenance."

She walked back to her desk and picked up the phone. "What extension?"

"I'm new. I can't remember. Can you look it up?" As he finished speaking, Brian heard voices coming from the inner office. One sounded like a woman's voice.

The secretary rolled her eyes. She nodded and opened her top drawer for the corporate directory. As she looked at the directory, Brian reached into his shirt pocket and hit a button. The secretary had just found the number for the maintenance department when Michaels Hayward's door opened. Brian quickly walked inside.

Brian stopped inside the office. The room was enormous. To his right was a conversation area made up of a sofa and over-stuffed chairs. To his left, a massive fireplace of green marble took up half the wall. Straight ahead, but about twenty feet away, a man sat behind a desk, looking up at him. His salt-and-pepper hair and mustache and prominent features gave him the look of an aristocrat.

He furrowed his brow. "Can I help you?" His words exuded confidence and control.

Brian stared at him for a moment and then said, "It took me a while, but I found you."

"You found me?" Michael asked with a raised eyebrow.

"You still don't know who I am, do you?" Brian asked.

Michael regarded him curiously. "Judging by your shirt, I'd say you're Willie."

The secretary was suddenly beside Brian. She spoke in a stern but controlled voice, a voice that he was sure was the right one. "Sir, you'll have to leave."

Brian didn't move. He stared hard at Michael.

"It's okay, Sheila," said Michael without taking his eyes off Brian. He gave her a nod, and she turned and walked from the room, giving Brian an incredulous look as she passed.

"Let me know if you want me to call security," she said.

"I'm a busy man, Willie. How can I help you?" Michael asked him.

"You son of a bitch! The name's not Willie. It's Brian Madsen. You know it well."

Michael was caught off guard. A look of panic came over him and then just as quickly disappeared as he regained control. "What can I do for you, Mr. Madsen? And why are you mas-querading as one of the building staff?"

Brian walked directly toward Michael, who stood and waited. Brian stopped and looked at the man across the massive desk. He felt a wave of anger from deep within him as he said, "You killed her. You murdering son of a bitch, you killed her to get to me! To get me to get to Jason Ross."

There was silence as they stared at one another, Brian in anger and Michael evaluating him.

"You killed her for a fucking job?" Brian shouted.

Michael didn't look away as he said, "I don't know what you're talking about."

Brian hit the desk with a fist. "Cathy Jenkins, someone who never harmed you. Your battle with Jason Ross. Your phone calls to me. I know your voice, and I know your game." Brian reached into one of the pockets of his overalls and pulled out the Saturday night special he was supposed to have used on Jason. He threw it loudly on the desk and then pointed at Michael. "You're going to jail, you bastard!"

Michael slowly shook his head and then said calmly, "Me? You said it yourself. She never harmed me, and I had no motive to hurt her. Besides, who was hiding an affair? Whose fingerprints are on the murder weapon, which the media tells me is in the possession of the police now? Seems to me that you're living on borrowed time."

Brian didn't hesitate as he said, "It won't work. The police will know everything. I'll admit to the affair, but the phone calls were yours. I know it, and my wife knows it." He thought he detected a grin on Michael's face, but he kept talking. "And someone else knows it." Brian thought of the woman who had called him back, the secretary outside the door. "I know that at least one of the calls was made from right here. Isn't that right?"

He watched the grin disappear and Michael's expression transform to one of concern. "You made a mistake, Hayward. You left a couple of loose ends that you can't talk around."

Michael hesitated. Then to Brian's surprise, he grinned more widely than before. "It won't happen like that, Brian." It was the same threatening and confident voice he had heard so many times on the telephone. "Even you won't testify against me."

Brian was now convinced that the man had lost his grip on reality. "You're done fucking around with people's lives. You're going away for a long time." He felt a sense of relief overtaking him. He had the killer, and he had the man before the police closed in on him.

Michael shook his head. "No, I'm not, Brian. At least not alone."

Brian's confidence dwindled, and he asked shakily, "What does that mean?"

"It means that, if I go to jail, your wife goes too."

"What?" Brian asked. His confusion was evident from his expression.

The bathroom door on the far side of the office opened, and Barbara stepped into the room. She looked at Brian and then at Michael. Sadness was in her eyes, but she didn't speak. Brian stared at her, waiting for some explanation.

Michael spoke first, "Ask her, Brian. She'll tell you about it. Your wife's been in on it from the beginning."

Brian looked at Barbara, waiting for a denial. She wouldn't look at him. He suddenly felt sick. His knees weakened, and for a moment, he felt that they might not hold his weight.

Michael watched him reeling. "You see, Brian, Barbara and I met at the inauguration. It was shortly after I saw you and Ms. Jenkins upstairs in the bathroom. At first, Barbara just needed a friend to talk to, to help her deal with a disloyal husband. But we soon discovered we had certain mutual needs."

Barbara spoke for the first time in angry tones, "Shut up, Michael." She still didn't look at Brian.

Michael ignored her. "I needed Jason Ross out of this company. Barbara needed Cathy Jenkins out of your lives." He drew a breath. "Not at first. It took a while. When I first told her what I'd seen upstairs, she was sick about it, but she was convinced it was a one-time mistake that wouldn't go any further. She had faith in you, Brian. Then when you kept it going—-" Michael raised his arms in a shrugging gesture. "She had to satisfy herself that there was no other way. When she followed you to the beach, well, that's what did it. Anyway, she had to stop the affair." Michael sat in his chair, leaning back comfortably with hands locked together behind his head.

Brian felt like he might fall down and had to hold on to the outer edge of the desk to steady himself. He looked over at Barbara, waiting for her to tell him it wasn't true or to offer some explanation. Silently she stared straight ahead in Michael's direction.

"Anyway," said Michael, "it's time you knew all about it, just to make sure you stay quiet." He spoke slowly and calmly. "So Barbara got what she wanted. Cathy Jenkins was out of your lives. You were supposed to do what I needed. Then it would all be over." He shook his head and smiled. "I never thought you'd hold out through all of it. Your wife should be credited with some great ideas, Brian. The car explosion? That was hers. A gem, don't you think?"

He slapped the desk and nodded in admiration of the feat. Michael stood and leaned over the desk toward Brian. "So you see, it's something of a standoff. You're not going to accuse me of anything unless you're okay with the idea of your wife spending the rest of her life in jail."

Brian looked over at Barbara's profile. "All of it?" He shook his head involuntarily. "Killing her? Setting me up as the killer? Making me think a car bomb almost killed you? And Lindsay. Oh God, Barbara, you almost killed Lindsay."

She looked at him for the first time with a pained expression on her face. "You weren't going to be set up as a killer. You were going to be protected. Everything that linked you to her was taken so that you would never be accused. And no one was supposed to get hurt—-"

"What's wrong with you? You killed a person and wanted to kill another. And nobody's supposed to be hurt? Your niece was just released from the hospital, and they're still not sure there won't be some permanent damage to her nervous system." Brian grabbed his face with both hands and closed his eyes. It was all a hideous nightmare. He opened his eyes, still facing Barbara. "And Bob. Where's he?"

Michael said, "Your friend was a problem. Something had to be done with him."

"Oh my God," Brian said again, feeling another wave of nausea. His head hurt. He could feel the blood rushing through his skull, like floodwaters about to overcome a dam. "You told him whatever I did," he said to Barbara with surprise and pain in his tone. "You called and told him when I called Bob and when I wanted to send you away in the rental car so you'd be safe. You made me think he was watching us ..." His voice trailed off into silence.

Barbara slowly nodded. A sad expression was on her face, and she spoke in a pleading tone. "I did it for us, Brian, to get you back." A tear was in her eye.

Brian's face flushed with anger. "For us? You killed a wonderful human being in a pact with this wacko son of a bitch for us? Just to get what you both wanted?" He looked at Michael. "You sent them the murder weapon with my fingerprints on it. So now I get arrested and prosecuted for Cathy's murder while you just watch?"

"Of course, you could have prevented that simply by doing what you were supposed to do." Michael grinned devilishly. "As a matter of fact, Barbara was here protesting the fact that I sent in your fingerprints when you arrived."

Barbara said angrily, "You son of a bitch, you were never supposed to set him up! We agreed that you wouldn't really use any of the evidence against Brian."

Michael turned to Brian. "That was before he let me down." He then regarded Barbara. "You got what you wanted. I saw to it. I got nothing. I needed a little insurance. When it became clear he wouldn't do it, something had to be done to make sure it didn't all unravel. I had to be sure the two of you didn't decide to lay all this on me." Michael raised his hands to gesture that it was only fair. "If you think about it, you'll see I had no choice."

Brian was silent. He thought about Barbara plotting to kill Cathy, and his heart hurt more than it ever had in his life. He thought about Barbara accepting his confession of infidelity, angrily at first and then forgivingly. He thought about her telling him to call the police when Michael's calls came in, knowing he wouldn't, knowing just how far to go. Then he thought about the tape recorder in his breast pocket, still running.

Amongst the whirlwind of thoughts, he hadn't noticed Barbara move over next to him. His mind was still racing as he noticed her reach toward the desk and pick up the gun he had thrown there, the gun he was to use on Jason Ross. She pointed the gun at Michael.

Brian opened his mouth and raised a hand to tell her to stop. Before he got a word out, she fired. The bullet entered Michael's chest and moved him backward in the chair. She fired again, the second bullet piercing his throat just above his Adam's apple. Michael grabbed at his neck with both hands as a fountain of blood erupted into the air. He struggled for breath, clawing at his throat and gasping. There were gurgling sounds as the blood overwhelmed his throat and lungs, and he fell to the floor, dead.

Barbara dropped the gun on the desk and turned to Brian. She spoke calmly and coherently, "We figured out who was blackmailing you and came to see him. You borrowed that outfit just in case they wouldn't let us in any other way. But he let us in. We confronted him with what we knew, and he panicked. He pulled the gun. You and he struggled, and the gun fell. I grabbed it and shot him."

Brian was too shocked to speak or even to acknowledge that he had heard her. He saw Barbara look down at the body. The flow of blood from the neck was now at a trickle. The green carpet was stained dark in wide circles around the body. Brian closed his eyes and then fell to his knees and vomited.

Chapter 22

People were all around Brian, someone asking if he were okay. Brian nodded weakly. He could hear the sound of sirens, a faint echo at first and then becoming an unremitting wail as they drew near. How long had it been since the shooting? Two minutes? Five minutes? He had no idea. He climbed to his feet with help from one of the new faces in the office. No one asked questions. No one walked over to where Michael lay, expelling what blood he had left onto the ever-widening black circle on the rug.

Brian thought about the recorder in his pocket and made an immediate decision. "I need to go to the bathroom," he told whoever stood beside him. "I'll be right back." He walked over to the bathroom and closed the door. He pulled out the recorder and dropped the microcassette into the toilet. Then he flushed it. He took the miniature recorder and wiped it clean of fingerprints. Then he placed it in one of the bathroom drawers, touching it only with the tissue.

When Brian returned to the turmoil in Michael's office, he sat down on the couch and put his head in his hands. Barbara sat down next to him, but neither spoke. He could hear the murmurs of the bystanders, some speculating about what might have happened, while others recoiled in horror at the sight on the floor. No one asked Brian or Barbara what had happened. Peering through his hands, Brian could see Sheila across the room, crying onto the shoulder of a coworker. Amongst it all, he felt bad for her.

Within two minutes, four uniformed officers stood at the door to the office with guns drawn, as someone near the door identified Brian and Barbara as being involved in the shooting.

The officer in front yelled, "Police! Hands on your heads."

Brian and Barbara both obliged.

"Everyone else into the outer office and wait for an officer to speak to you. Touch nothing in here," the officer commanded.

Two of the officers had Brian stand, put handcuffs on him, and told him to sit back down. They then did the same to Barbara.

Within three minutes, other police officers arrived. Uniformed officers received directions that sent them out of Michael's office and out of Brian's view. Paramedics rolled in a gurney and prepared to remove the body. Technicians arrived and poured over the scene, photographing Michael's body and examining the surrounding outpourings of blood. They began looking at everything in the room but moved nothing. Brian still sat on the couch, his body shaking with the shock of the events that had befallen him, silently watching this forensic world that had been set irreversibly into motion.

He couldn't bring himself to look at Barbara, who sat next to him silently. He knew she periodically looked over at him for what he speculated would be confirmation that he would describe the events leading to Michael's death as she had laid them out. Brian took deep breaths, trying to hang onto what little control of his emotions he had left. His stomach muscles had knotted over waves of nausea. His head pounded as he felt the blood rushing to it and seemingly never leaving. He felt the droplets of water on his brow, though his body wasn't hot.

Brian put his elbows on his knees and leaned forward, resting his chin in both hands. He stared down at the floor. Feelings of sadness and loss swept over him. He fought to suppress the feelings of anger that rose inside. He wouldn't allow himself to think about Barbara and what she had done. He feared it would come out as he spoke to the police, and there was a larger fear that he would not be able to cope with those new realities.

Brian looked up to see the familiar faces of Merrick and Palmer, who were watching him with deadpan expressions. For the first time, Brian looked over at Barbara, who stared straight ahead, seemingly lost in thought.

"Mr. Madsen, you okay?"

Brian nodded. He meant to say something, but no words came out.

Merrick directed that the handcuffs be removed from Brian and Barbara. One of the uniformed officers quickly pulled out his key and removed them. Merrick looked pointedly at Brian. "I'd like you to come with me, sir."

Brian mechanically stood and began to follow Merrick and Palmer from the room, as did Barbara.

Merrick looked at Barbara. "Not you, Mrs. Madsen. If you'll wait right here for just a minute, Detectives Wagner and Lane will be along to speak with you. They're the two plainclothes officers over by the desk."

Barbara suddenly looked worried. "But I want to stay with my husband. This is a very stressful time, and I ..." She let her words trail off.

"Let me assure you that we are aware of that, ma'am. But we have procedures we have to follow when investigating a homicide."

She visibly cringed and then sat down on the couch. Brian suddenly felt tired and very alone. Merrick gestured that Brian follow with a wave of his hand, and they walked from the room. Palmer followed behind Brian as they walked through the mass of humanity in the outer office. Several uniformed officers interviewed bystanders. One was speaking with Sheila, who held a tissue to her eyes. Brian felt a desperate urge to speak to her, to share what they knew about Michael. He felt a bonding born of shared tragedy to this woman he didn't even know. It occurred to him that maybe he needed a friend.

Brian's walk down the same corridor he had used to get to Michael's office had an entirely different feel to it. A familiar, last-mile quality that he had often feared as walls of threats and incriminating evidence had closed in on him. Somehow he wasn't scared, just lonelier than he had ever felt, numbed by a compounded sense of loss too horrible to bear. He wouldn't allow himself to dwell on Barbara's role in Cathy's death or in setting him up as her killer. It was all too heartless, too inhuman, to comprehend. He lacked the mental strength to withstand such obsession. At the same time, he knew that such thoughts could not be avoided, only deferred.

Brian followed Merrick into a conference room, where Merrick pointed to a chair at the end of a long table. Brian sat down, staring straight ahead as Merrick and Palmer took seats on either side of him.

"Mr. Madsen," Merrick began, "I'm going to record our conversation." Merrick placed a tape recorder on the table between them. He pushed a button on the machine, assured himself that it was properly running, and then said, "Mr. Madsen, you are under arrest. We're going to read you your rights at this point before we go any further."

Taking a small plastic card from his pocket, he began to read without waiting for a response from Brian. "You are under arrest for the murder of Cathy Jenkins. You have the right to remain silent. You have the right to legal counsel before questioning. If you wish but cannot afford legal counsel, one will be appointed for you. If you elect to waive these rights, anything you say can and will be used against you in a court of law. Do you understand each of these rights as I have explained them to you?"

Brian nodded. "I understand. But I didn't kill Cathy."

"Excuse me, Mr. Madsen, we're not quite done. Do you wish to waive these rights and answer questions about the deaths of

Cathy Jenkins and Michael Hayward without the presence of counsel?"

"I do. I didn't kill Cathy. He did." Brian gestured toward Michael's office.

Merrick regarded him closely before responding, "We obtained the warrant for your arrest for the murder of Cathy Jenkins based, in part, on the fact that we now have what has been confirmed as the murder weapon with your fingerprints all over it."

Brian nodded. "I know that. I was set up. He blackmailed me." He motioned again in Michael's direction.

Merrick sat back in his seat and looked at Brian, as if analyzing him. It was the expression of a man who sifted through bullshit for a living, listening with his eyes for Brian wasn't sure what. *Evasion? Inconsistency of words and expression? Some unidentifiable manifestation of guilt in my words, face, or movements that would convict me before I left this room?* It was a moment devoid of time. Brian couldn't tell if the silence had consumed only seconds or many minutes.

"Why don't you tell us about it?" Merrick finally said.

"It's a long story," Brian said, unsure of where to begin.

Merrick nodded. "We have time."

Brian drew in a deep breath and then said, "I had an affair with Cathy Jenkins. It began the night of my inaugural party and continued until ... until she died. I had been with her that night. I got home at about one and went to bed. When I got up in the morning, it was all over the news." He noted Merrick's eyes, fixed upon him, conveying nothing. "I cared about Cathy, and my wife didn't know anything about the affair. I was still trying to cope with the news, and what I should do when his first call came in."

Brian briefly cupped his hands over his mouth. He noticed his breathing had grown faster. "Hayward knew about Cathy and me. He told me that Cathy's apartment had been stripped of traces of my presence. He told me he had taken objects from the apartment that contained my fingerprints, but if I cooperated with him, they would never find their way to the police."

Brian studied the face that was devoid of expression and said softly, "Jesus, I wish I'd handled it differently. I put him in total control, right from the start. Then there was no way back." Brian looked down at his shoes but didn't stop talking. "He said I must kill someone for him, or Cathy's murder weapon would go to you guys. And that's what happened. I just couldn't do it."

He looked at Merrick and shook his head. "I actually thought I might, especially when my family's safety was threatened. Then there was the car bomb. You remember that? It's because I was balking. He did it to convince me he'd kill my family if I didn't go through with it."

Brian momentarily rested his head in his hands. Then he suddenly looked up at Merrick. "Bob Galvin. Have you heard anything about him? Can you find him?"

"Who's Bob Galvin?" Merrick asked with narrowed eyes.

"He's a private investigator and a buddy of mine. I called him to help me find the caller. That son of a bitch did something to him. He said something about it today." Brian leaned back in his chair. "What did I do to him?"

"We'll check on him," Merrick said, and he dispatched Palmer with a nod. After Palmer left the room, Merrick asked, "So how did you know your caller was Hayward?"

"I met with Jason Ross after I learned Jason was the one I was supposed to kill." He left out the specifics of their meeting in the garage. "Jason gave me a list of three who had serious grudges against him. Hayward was on the list. What really did it though was his secretary. Once after he called, she called back. Apparently she heard some of it and wanted to know what it was all about. Then she changed her mind and hung up.

"When I got here today, I recognized her voice. Then Hayward acknowledged it all. He said there was no way we'd prove it, that my fingerprints were on the murder weapon that he had already delivered to the police. He said he didn't even know Cathy Jenkins and had no motive to kill her and asserted that I had a secret affair to cover."

"So you killed him?" Merrick asked almost casually.

"No." Brian looked down again.

"Your wife killed him?" Merrick said after a moment.

Brian nodded and then added, "But it was self-defense. More accurately, defense of both of us. Hayward pulled out the gun. I struggled with him, and she managed to come up with it and fired to stop him."

Merrick studied him carefully. "There's a number of things that you haven't been honest about in the past," Merrick said pointedly. "Like never seeing Cathy Jenkins socially. Remember?"

"Yes, I remember. I just felt so trapped," Brian said desperately. "I thought I had no choice. Between the blackmailer threatening to turn over evidence and threats to my family ..." His voice trailed off.

Merrick nodded and gave him an understanding look. Brian could feel that the man accepted his statement as truth, the true parts and the rest. "We'll check out what you've said. It'll be up to the district attorney to decide whether there's a prosecution. But if you're telling the truth, and I think you are, I'll recommend against it. In the meantime, I'm going to have to take you in and book you for the murder."

He waved the warrant in explanation. "The warrant is because your fingerprints are all over the weapon that killed Ms. Jenkins. If your story checks out, this won't go too far." He paused. "You lied to us about how well you knew Ms. Jenkins, but given your marital and political situation—-not that I think it was a smart idea, mind you—-I can see how that happened." He stood up and signaled Brian to do the same. "One more thing.

Get a good lawyer to make sure everything goes right and that you get out sooner rather than later."

The police escorted Brian from the building in handcuffs. The hallways had been largely cleared of onlookers, though uniformed officers were intermittently stationed while investigators worked the site. There was no sign of Barbara, and the door to Michael's office was now closed. When they walked out of the building, the sudden darkness struck Brian. It seemed darker and colder than usual. A sense of foreboding confronted him.

A voice softly said something he couldn't make out. Then someone pushed down on his head and guided him into the back seat of a police cruiser. Unfamiliar faces watched as he was driven away.

In his mind, Brian saw Cathy's warm smile and thought about how much she had loved him. He had known how much she cared from the beginning, but he had not wanted to deal with it. He had seen it only as a complicating issue. Now with the sudden shock of a mortal wound, he wanted to tell her how wonderful she had been, but he acknowledged to himself that he would never get that chance.

Brian leaned back against the seat and closed his eyes. He saw Barbara standing in Michael's office, denying nothing and never looking at him. Then he saw her with the gun as Michael fell to the floor, a look of stunned disbelief overtaking him, trying to figure out what had happened even as he was dying.

Brian was booked, photographed, and fingerprinted. Then he was permitted to make a phone call. He called one of his former law partners, who he was sure would know a good criminal lawyer. Brian was assured that he would be contacted in the morning. After his call, a guard escorted him down a long corridor of metal compartments. He was taken to a cell that contained a single bed, a small sink, and a toilet. Brian's handcuffs were removed, and he was moved inside. He looked at the fourteen-foot square room, bereft of all decoration, and heard the metal on metal sound of the doors being closed behind him.

He lay down on the bed and looked around this foreign world, hearing the words and movements of other occupants in the distance. Brian closed his eyes. He knew there was no chance of sleep, wanting only a few moments of peace from the graphic images of death that pervaded his thoughts.

Chapter 23

Brian drifted a few times, finding refuge from his thoughts, but he never really slept. In the morning, he was told that Barbara had been there but was not allowed to see him yet. At eight o'clock, he was informed that an attorney, Lloyd Martin, was there to meet with him. He was taken to a small room with two chairs and a table at its center. A tall, thin man with thick gray hair that was almost white waited for Brian's escort to leave before speaking. He wore an expensive suit and wire-rimmed glasses. There was a stately quality to the way the man carried himself. He held a briefcase at his side. The effect was something between IRS auditor and television commentator.

"I'm Lloyd Martin," the man said, extending a hand to Brian.

Brian awkwardly shook it with still-cuffed hands, briefly nodding. Each took a chair as the guard closed the door behind them.

Lloyd opened his case and pulled out a notepad. He wasted no time. "So tell me the whole story. I'll tell you if it sells."

Brian spoke of his affair with Cathy and of being at home with Barbara at the time of the murder. He went through as many of Michael's calls as he could remember. He talked about the call back from the woman he now knew was Michael's secretary. Lloyd seemed to like that fact, twice underlining the note and placing an asterisk in the margin.

Brian told him about meeting with Jason Ross and trying to find out who would want Jason dead. He told of the list of names he had gotten from Jason and making his way down the list to Michael. Lloyd seemed to like that part too, again marking his notes. Brian told him about obtaining the custodian's uniform to walk into the building and up to the executive floors without detection so he could confront Michael by surprise. He told Lloyd about Michael's admission and his insistence that Brian remain the suspect in order for the affair to be concealed.

Lloyd sat back in his chair, tapping his pen against his notepad as he reflected. "I took the liberty of talking to Barbara because I saw her out front."

Brian nodded, unsure of what to say.

"What I'm not clear on is where Hayward got the gun and why he produced it at all. I mean, he thought you were still the prime suspect, right? So why pull a gun in your own office?"

Brian nodded thoughtfully and fidgeted uncomfortably, hoping his nervousness wasn't detectable to Lloyd. "He seemed to get the gun from in or on his desk; I'm not sure which. As to why, I guess it was panic. I told him about the call back from his secretary and that I knew he had made one or more of the calls from his office. I could see it was true in his eyes. I think he panicked."

Lloyd reflected for a moment and then nodded, apparently satisfied. "I've set the wheels in motion. You'll appear before a judge tomorrow morning, and by then, I expect to have enough put together to make sure bail is granted." He stood and shook Brian's hand once more.

"Thank you, Mr. Martin. I really appreciate that."

Lloyd called for the guard to let him out and then shook Brian's hand again. "I know you've never been stuck in this kind of a place. Has to scare the shit out of you. But don't worry. We'll get you out of here."

Brian nodded as Lloyd walked quickly out the door.

At nine thirty the next morning, Brian was on his way home. He had entered a plea of not guilty and was released on fifty thousand dollars bail after a fifteen-minute hearing. A conversation in the judge's chambers consumed ten minutes of the hearing, during which Lloyd carefully described Brian's background, character, and the facts depicting him as Michael's victim.

The prosecutor, who appeared seasoned by comfort level and knowledge, seemed fully apprised of the facts and offered no disagreement. When Lloyd had finished, the judge released Brian with an apology that the bail was so high, explaining that, in a capital case, it was required. Brian thanked the judge for his understanding, and he was soon on the street thanking Lloyd, who said he would be in touch within the next couple of days.

Barbara had been waiting in the courtroom. She drove Brian home, expressing her happiness at his release. Brian did little more than acknowledge her and was silent for most of the ride. When they got home, she parked the car and then hugged him and held on tightly. He sat motionless.

"Let's go inside." Brian heard the icy chill of his own words, but there was no way he could make it sound differently.

Brian walked into the living room and then turned to look at Barbara. He stared at her, conveying anger and disbelief in the same fiery expression.

"I did it for us, Brian," she said when she saw his glare. "Don't you understand? I did it to save us." She spoke the words in desperation, as if they otherwise might not be heard. "You were going to throw away everything we had."

"How could you be part of killing her? Of framing me for murder? You set me up to murder a stranger, to make me a killer too. Jesus, Barbara, it's monstrous! What about Lindsay?"

"I had to get you back, Brian. You don't know how it feels to lose the only person you've ever loved. I was losing you to her." Her eyes began to cloud over with tears. "Did you love her?"

"I don't know. But I cared about her." He put his hands on his face and then pushed them up and back through his hair. "And you killed her, just as surely as if you pulled the trigger yourself."

"I love you," she said, choking on her tears. "This is all because I loved you so much that I couldn't let her take you away from me and everything we spent our whole lives building. Can't you see that?" Uncontrollable sobs punctuated her words.

Brian was silent for a few moments and then said softly, "No, Barbara, I can't see that. I just don't understand how you thought murder and blackmail could bring me closer to you. How could you think that what you and Michael did would make things all right?"

He left her crying and walked outside on the patio. The sense of tranquility that usually awaited him in the seclusion of the patio was nowhere to be found. The sky was overcast. The bulging pillows of black clouds were ominously threatening. The usual array of singing birds was deafeningly silent. Brian had never felt so alone.

Brian sat in the stillness, staring out into the blackness of the night punctuated only by sporadic lights at various distances that cast hypnotic rays at his eyes. He didn't know how long he had been sitting alone when he felt Barbara's hand on his arm. He didn't pull away. He just turned slowly to look at her face, suddenly noticing the sadness in those eyes that had been a part of him for so long. He felt a deep despair. He put his hand on hers and looked away, back out into the dark night sky.

"Brian." She paused until he turned to look at her. "I'm sorry, but I have to ask you about what happened when they questioned you."

He looked at her quizzically.

"What did you tell them? About me, I mean."

"Just what you suggested," he said harshly. "He pulled the gun, I struggled with him, the gun somehow came loose, and you used it to protect us."

She let out a deep breath and nodded, squeezing his arm. It hadn't occurred to him until then. She had been worried that he had implicated her. It must have been a tough thirty-six hours for her.

"There were a couple of things that we never discussed. Like the gun, they asked me where it came from," she said.

Brian nodded. "They asked me that too. I told them that he got it from on or in his desk, but I didn't know which. I said it happened too quickly."

She nodded concurrence. "One other thing. What about how we got there and who got there first?"

"I told them I used the maintenance uniform to get in, that I went there alone and you showed up just a few minutes later."

She sat down and leaned back in the chair.

"Does that work? I mean, is it consistent with what you said?" Brian asked.

"Yes, it works. I told them I saw you walk in and followed." She put her hand on his. "Thank you, Brian."

He nodded briefly and then returned to surveying the darkness.

Chapter 24

Brian lay on the couch around two in the morning. His fitful sleep didn't begin until almost four. Disquieting dreams of amorphous shadows lying in wait and faceless attackers stalking the unsuspecting interrupted his sleep. He woke up sweating with the ringing of the telephone working its way into his consciousness. He glanced at his watch. It was eight thirty.

"Hello?" Brian said in raspy, morning voice tones.

"Brian? This is Lloyd Martin."

There was a click and a greeting from Barbara on the upstairs line.

"I'm glad you're both on. I've got some news," Lloyd said.

"What is it?" Brian asked anxiously.

"I think we can eliminate any possibility of charges against either of you and get the whole thing wrapped up quickly."

"Really?" Barbara asked with excitement in her voice.

Somehow that familiar tone made Brian feel saddened. He had no idea why.

Lloyd continued, "Ray Fernandez is on the case at the DA's office. We went to law school together and have a good relationship. He's a smart guy and a good prosecutor, but he's reasonable. He invited us over this afternoon to have you tell him the story. He already thinks you guys are clean and there should be no charges." Lloyd paused to let his words sink in. "So if you're up for telling it again, we have a two o'clock appointment."

"We're up for it," Barbara said.

"Brian?" Lloyd asked.

"Sure," he replied after a moment.

"I'll let them know we're on and meet you there at two," Lloyd said. "Anything else I should know before we go?"

Barbara was quick to respond, "I can't think of anything."

"No, nothing," Brian added unconvincingly.

"Good. I'll see you there."

Lloyd was waiting for Brian in Barbara in the lobby of the DA's office when they arrived at two o'clock. They shook hands. Then Lloyd turned to a secretary who sat behind a waist-high partition. "We're all here."

She gave him a smile. "Okay, Mr. Martin, please follow me." She stood and turned to a door behind her. There was a buzzing sound, and she pulled open the door. She led them down a long corridor to a conference room.

Most of the room was taken by a large oval table, surrounded by six swivel chairs. A short Hispanic man with thinning black hair and a black mustache stood to greet them. He smiled widely as Lloyd introduced them. The man defied the tough-guy prosecutor image.

"Good afternoon, Mr. and Mrs. Madsen," he said warmly.

Ray was pleasant, disarming, and unthreatening. He made a point of making sure everyone had coffee and a modicum of small talk before moving on to more pressing subjects. He had deep-set green eyes that emitted kindness as well as intelligence.

"Just for the completeness of my notes, I would like to hear the whole story from Mr. Madsen." His tone was encouraging, as if they were friends chatting over afternoon tea.

As Brian spoke, Ray listened carefully, asked questions at logical breaks, and allowed Lloyd the opportunity to add or clarify on their behalves as he deemed fit. Ray nodded supportively as details were forthcoming. Occasionally he added acknowledgment of how hard it all must have been, for Brian being a likely suspect in a brutal murder and for both of them dealing with the blackmailer.

When they finished speaking, he had the coffee cups refilled and then said, "I'm sorry for all you've been through. We'll try not to make it any more burdensome than it has to be from this point." He paused briefly. "I can tell you that we've confirmed that Michael was your blackmailer. We confirmed that one of the calls to your house came from Michael's office. We've also had a helpful conversation with his secretary."

Ray smiled warmly. "I just want you to know that we already have support for what you're saying. Anyway I expect little difficulty in promptly completing the investigation and clearing you both of all charges without much inconvenience."

He thanked them for coming and walked them to the door. Ray and Lloyd shook hands and exchanged pleasantries about their families. Then there was a final round of good-byes, like old friends parting company as they reached the door.

Once outside, Lloyd smiled and shook hands with Brian and Barbara. "Nothing left to do now but wait for confirmation that all charges are being dropped. You saw how it went in there. I think it will all be done within the next few days."

They thanked Lloyd and then walked to the car in silence.

At four thirty, the telephone rang. Brian came in from the patio, where he had spent the bulk of the day since leaving Lloyd, and picked up the phone. "Hello?"

"Mr. Madsen?" It was a male voice he couldn't place.

"Yes?"

"This is Officer Palmer."

"How can I help you, Officer?" Brian felt his stomach knotting.

"Sergeant Merrick asked me to give you a call and let you know we've got some good news. We found your friend Bob. He's alive."

Brian leaned forward for the first time in too many days, feeling the rush that comes from something good. "Where is he?"

"He's in Westside Hospital. Been there a couple of days."

"How bad is he hurt?"

"He's stable and doing well. Couple of broken ribs, left arm and right leg broken, the leg in a couple of places, concussion, and a lot of lacerations and abrasions. We'd have found him sooner except he was admitted without identification and he was unconscious."

"Thanks for the call and for finding him. I'm on my way over there," Brian said quickly.

He hung up and yelled across the house, "Barb! They found Bob. He's going to be okay." He grabbed his coat from the hall closet as she came into view. "I'm going to the hospital to see him." Brian regarded her somber look. "You want to go along?"

She nodded. "Yes, I want to see him. Thank God he's alive." A sob came from deep inside her, and she began to cry uncontrollably.

Brian walked over and put his arms around her. She sobbed uncontrollably from the guilt, the relief, and the regret of everything she couldn't undo.

* * *

Brian walked into the hospital room and searched for Bob's bed. Bob's eyes found Brian at the same time he saw and surveyed his friend, bandaged seemingly from head to foot. His right leg was in a cast and hoist into the air on a system of cables and pulleys. His left arm was casted and bound to his chest. A bandage reached across his abdomen from chest to waistline, and another covered his forehead. Scratches, tears, and bruises adorned his face. Brian walked over to Bob and hugged his head, conscious of the fact that any touching might hurt given his condition.

"Ouch," Bob whispered.

"That's it? Ouch? I've been looking for you in every sleazy place in town, and all I get is ouch," Brian said jokingly.

Bob let out a pained laugh. "You were just a little premature. I'm going to those places next." He let out a laugh and then a grimace at the pain it caused him. "Damn, broken ribs aren't good for your sense of humor. Hi, Barb. You okay?" He made a reaching gesture with his better hand.

She touched the hand softly. "I'm fine, Bob. Much better now that I know you're going to make it."

Brian sat in a chair beside the bed. "What happened?"

"First, what happened to you guys? Someone was seriously out to do some harm," Bob said weakly.

Barbara opened her mouth to speak, but Brian spoke first, "We figured out who the blackmailer was. We confronted him, and he's dead."

"Jesus. You don't mess around."

"What happened to you, buddy?" Brian touched Bob's hand gently.

Bob shook his head as best he could. "It's too damned embarrassing to talk about."

"Embarrassing?"

"Yeah, the client catches the bad guy while I get the shit beat out of me."

"That happens from time to time in your job, right?"

"Not like this. I think I'll leave this one off my résumé. Unfucking-believable."

Brian grinned. "Tell me already."

"First day I took on your job, well, you know it wasn't just another case. I had a friend who needed the skills I had, so I wanted to go all out. Nail the son of a bitch and give you guys some relief. I make calls to my office to get the investigation underway. I decide I'm going to stop at my place, change, and then go see what's his name. Jason Ross. I walk into my house reading the mail, oblivious to the signs of a break-in at my own house that I'm trained to be on the lookout for anytime I enter anywhere. I'm inside maybe ten seconds when I get zapped with something, and down I go. Next thing I remember, I'm tied up and gagged in a small, dark closet I don't know where by I don't know who."

Brian smiled. "That could have happened to anyone—-"

"Maybe so, but I'm not done yet. It gets worse." He moved his chin awkwardly. "Brian, you want to scratch my left shoulder. It's driving me nuts."

Brian scratched softly and heard a groan of relief.

Then Bob continued, "Anyway I start working on the ropes that are binding my hands behind me. I'm rubbing them against a not-too-sharp doorjamb, so this is a big project. Maybe eight or nine hours go by. I'm just about loose when the door opens and he sees me moving. He hits me again. I'm out cold again."

Brian smiled.

"Yeah, real funny shit. Anyway, I wake up I don't know how much later. There's another rope, and it's tighter than ever. I start working at it again. I finally get loose, untie myself, and work my way out of the closet. I'm in this lakeside cabin all alone. I go outside and look around, but there's nothing but woods and lake in most directions. I see some tire tracks, so figuring it's my best shot at finding something else, I follow them. A few miles and it becomes a bad road. I take that a couple more miles and find a general store with a pay phone outside. I go inside and figure out where I am. Then I call the police to get some help.

"At this point I'm feeling some relief. I hang up the phone knowing that they're on the way, turn back toward the store, and see a car coming at me. It's maybe fifteen feet away and coming fast. I make a move to get out of the way, but by now we know it's not my day. Last thing I remember is going up on the hood. I wake up here," he said and looked down at himself, "in my present condition." He shook his head. "Any questions?"

Brian nodded. "Just one. Am I going to get a big bill for this?"

"Damned straight. I told you my per diem was plus expenses, right?" Bob waved his arm to the surrounding room, and they all broke into laughter.

Chapter 25

The night of his visit to see Bob in the hospital, Brian slept better. He had taken to staying awake long into the night and then falling asleep whenever he could on the couch. He awoke at seven and made his way to the kitchen. He started the coffee and then sat down in the dining room to wait. The loud ring of the telephone broke the morning silence. Brian picked it up on the second ring and mumbled a greeting.

"Brian." The voice paused for only a moment. "Lloyd Martin."

"Hi, Lloyd."

There was a long, ominous silence. Lloyd said, "There's some important news I have to share with you. Do you want me to come over?"

"No, tell us on the phone. I'll get Barb on the line." Brian put down the phone and walked to the bottom of the stairs. "Barbara, you awake?"

"Yes, I'm awake," came the groggy reply.

"Pick up the extension. Lloyd Martin has news." Brian returned to the phone and then waited for her greeting. "Okay, Lloyd, what is it?"

"You sure you don't want me to come over? It may be news better delivered in person."

"Just tell us, Lloyd. I can't wait while you drive over here," Barbara said impatiently.

"Brian?" Lloyd asked reluctantly.

"I agree. Tell us."

"Ray Fernandez just called me. There are no charges against Brian. They have enough evidence to know that Michael Hayward killed Cathy Jenkins to set up the blackmail. His secretary, Sheila Olsen, overheard one of the calls to you. She hit the automatic redial and got you on the telephone. Apparently, when you spoke with her, she panicked and hung up. Then she realized she had no way back to you."

Brian paused and drew a breath. "It all seems to fit. Cathy Jenkins must have been surprised when Michael Hayward showed up at her apartment in the middle of the night, but she knew he was one of the big shots at International Resource, so she let him in."

"Oh, God," Brian said. "Poor Cathy."

"You're definitely off the hook, Brian, notwithstanding the fingerprints on the murder weapon. The blackmail is pretty clear." He paused.

"And that's not the part you didn't want to say on the phone, right?" Brian prompted.

"Right." There was yet another pause, and this one Brian interpreted as Lloyd's search for the right words. Lloyd cleared his throat before continuing. "The news isn't so good where Barbara is concerned."

"What is it?" Barbara asked quickly. "They know he was killed in self-defense, right?" Urgency was in her voice.

"What's wrong?" Brian asked.

"Well, both of you said that Hayward pulled the gun on you in the office. Then there was a struggle. Barbara got hold of the gun and shot him, right?"

"Right," Barbara said.

"The first problem is that they interviewed Jason Ross, and he said that Brian pulled a gun on him. The gun was with Brian, not Michael."

"There's a lot of things that could account for that," Barbara said. "Two guns that look alike."

"Yeah, maybe. They were a little suspicious that no one said anything about a second gun, but we could have gotten around that one. There's a much bigger problem."

"What?" Barbara asked in a panicky voice.

"The investigation team went back to Hayward's office for another review of the scene. One of them happened to look in the toilet, and a microcassette tape was floating in the bowl. They brought it back to the lab and dried it out. I just saw a transcript."

"Oh my God," Barbara said softly.

"With the tape, they're going to charge Barbara with murder."

Barbara let out a shrill, pitiful cry that sounded to Brian like the desperate last sounds of a cornered animal. Brian listened silently, feeling his heart pounding.

"They know what you saw in that office, Brian," Lloyd said quietly. "So you don't want to say anything inconsistent with the tape, or you could face perjury or obstruction of justice charges. At the same time, you don't have to testify against your wife."

"But if I don't testify, I can't help Barbara," Brian said.

"And if you do testify, you won't help her at all because you're stuck with what was said on the tape before Hayward was shot."

There was a protracted silence before Brian asked, "What can you do about this, Lloyd?"

"Not a lot, I'm afraid. You know what was said in that room. There's not much ambiguity, and there's a great deal of admission. A jury won't have to deliberate long."

"So what are you saying?" Barbara asked, sounding a bit calmer.

"Just that we should think about making a deal ... if we can get it. Murder two or, best-case scenario, maybe even manslaughter. I'm sorry."

Brian asked softly, "So what do we do?"

Lloyd said, "Barbara has until five o'clock this evening to turn herself in. It goes down better that way. No patrol cars and no handcuffs. And it looks a lot more like cooperation in the newspapers."

Brian leaned back in his chair and closed his eyes. "Thanks, Lloyd. We'll call you by noon to make arrangements."

"That's fine. One more thing. Barbara, it's going to occur to you to run. Don't do it. If you do, they'll catch you, and then our deal-making leverage will be severely compromised."

"I understand," Barbara said.

Brian heard the click as she hung up and then said, "Thanks for doing what you can. I'll talk to you before noon."

He put the phone back in its cradle without waiting for a response and then turned toward the stairs. Barbara was walking down the last of them with her wide eyes glazed over.

"It had to end this way, didn't it?" she said.

Brian was silent.

"For a little while I really thought we were going to get past this. That they would never know. I thought it would die with Michael and then I could start earning your love again. I know I could have, if there were just enough time. I love you so much, Brian. Sooner or later I could have shown you."

He put his arms around her and held her tight. "I know, Barb. I know." He leaned back and looked into her eyes. "I'm so sorry about the tape. I thought it was gone."

Brian felt a deep sense of sorrow. He hadn't forgiven her and doubted he ever could. *Not for Cathy. Not after all that had happened.* Still, that had a history, and he didn't want Barbara to spend her life in a cell. *After hearing the tape, maybe they would know that she needed help, that psychiatric treatment and not jail was in order.* Somehow this thought brought him hope.

"It really is poetic justice, isn't it?" She twisted her expression into a thin, unhappy smile. "Is there a choice here? I mean, should I run?" There was a faint glimmer of hope in her eyes as she asked, "Would you go with me?" She sounded like a child, lost and hopeless.

Brian looked at her sadly and then shook his head. "No, Barb, I couldn't."

She nodded. "I understand." She turned and walked upstairs, looking back once to give Brian a smile and then disappearing down the hallway.

Brian and Barbara drove in silence to Lloyd Martin's office. The situation, not the silence, was the source of the overwhelming sense of loss Brian felt. Lloyd was awaiting their arrival. He told his secretary he wasn't sure when he would be back.

She nodded and flashed Barbara a sympathetic expression. "Take care," she said to Barbara, who nodded and walked to the door.

When they arrived at the police department downtown, Merrick, Palmer, and Ray Fernandez met them at the door. All of whom wore somber expressions as they were escorted inside. Brian found some comfort in the thought that none of this brought them pleasure. They were just doing a job, and it appeared that they would have preferred it had come out differently.

Brian looked over at Barbara. She stared straight ahead as she walked. No emotion was revealed in her expression. *She's in shock*, Brian thought. He took her hand and squeezed it as they walked.

They were directed to an office in the booking area, where Lloyd was the first to speak. "Barbara, the tape has been studied at length. Everyone knows what happened. I think you might benefit from some psychiatric care. None of these gentlemen disagree. If you're receptive and the doctors who examine you agree, it's even possible that your time spent may take the form of treatment rather than imprisonment. Would that be okay with you?"

She looked at him and smiled. "That would be fine, Lloyd. Can Brian come see me sometimes?"

He nodded. "I think so."

They gave Brian a few minutes to tell Barbara good-bye. She hugged him tightly until the officers came back into the room. Then she released him, kissed him on the cheek, and told him that she would always love him. She gave Brian a smile as she followed Merrick and Palmer from the room.

When Barbara was out of view, Lloyd turned to Brian. "She'll be arraigned tomorrow. We'll offer a diminished capacity plea on her behalf." He was silent for a moment and then asked, "Is there anything I can do for you?"

Brian shook his head. "Just do everything you can for Barbara." He felt a tear welling in the corner of his eye but didn't wipe it. "And thanks for caring."

After saying good-bye to Ray, Lloyd drove Brian back to his car in silence. They shook hands as Brian got out of the car.

Lloyd said, "Let me know if I can do anything … anything at all."

Brian smiled weakly. "You're doing it. Thanks."

As Brian drove toward home, it began to drizzle. He watched a young couple walking down the street, sharing an umbrella and laughing, and his tears began to fall. He grieved for all that had been lost, including the love of the woman who had always been his partner. She would be institutionalized or jailed, and he would stand by to support her.

He thought about Cathy, who had been a forbidden ray of sunshine. She too was lost to him, and there was no doubt in his mind that he was responsible for all of it. Everything stemmed from the sins of his inaugural and the man who had witnessed them. And he too was dead.

Brian closed his eyes and saw Cathy's smile. He thought about his plan to tell her good-bye, and he was glad he never did. Her final thoughts of him were of the future they would share. He wiped away a tear as he thought about all that might have been.

When Brian got home, he walked out onto the patio. The light rain had stopped, and he sat to watch the final moments of daylight fading away. The sun slowly disappeared from view, leaving splashes of orange and red on the horizon. He felt a sense of isolation and loneliness overtake him. Everyone important to him had paid the price for his sins. He considered the emptiness inside him and knew it was part of the price to be paid.

His atonement was just beginning. This was the first of many sunsets he would see alone, his only companion the haunting thoughts of love that had touched him and been taken away.

Chapter 26

The morning after Barbara's arrest, Brian sat at the counsel table in Department 316 as the thin-faced judge, who couldn't have been over forty by Brian's assessment, stared down at them over wire-rimmed glasses from his elevated vantage point behind the bench. The seal of the State of California was perched on the wall behind him, between the Stars and Stripes on one side and the prominent bear of the state flag on the other. Every seat in the courtroom, including the jury box, was occupied by the worried faces of defendants about to be arraigned, watching the judge attentively before he had uttered his first word, and lawyers clad in blue suits and red ties, displaying expressions of boredom or impatience.

Judge Alfred Byers looked up from the paperwork that had consumed him for the past few minutes and scanned the audience with concern, as if wondering if any of these people were armed or maybe just how long it would take to get through the calendar given the sheer numbers present. He then returned his eyes to the lawyers at the counsel table in front of him.

"The State of California versus Barbara Madsen," Judge Byers called out in a loud voice and then read an eleven- or twelve-digit number from a sheet in front of him. "Are the parties ready to proceed?" he asked in a perfunctory manner that suggested he didn't really care.

Lloyd Martin and the blond man Brian assumed was with the district attorney's office both stood.

"Garrett Gardner, ready for the people," the blond man delivered, as if proud of the alliteration his name presented.

Judge Byers looked unimpressed. "Mr. Gardner," he said with a brief nod.

"Lloyd Martin on behalf of Mrs. Madsen, Your Honor."

The judge acknowledged with another perfunctory nod. "We are ready to dispense with a formal reading of the charges and enter a plea?" Judge Byers asked.

"We are, Your Honor," Lloyd said with conviction.

There was a brief moment of silence while a look of impatience took hold of the judge's expression. "Well, don't keep me in suspense, counsel."

"Right, Your Honor," Lloyd replied. "Mrs. Madsen pleads not guilty."

"Fine. The record will so reflect. This matter is set over for preliminary hearing." Judge Byers paused while he squinted to look at a large wall calendar fifteen feet away. "Four weeks from today." He looked to the attorneys, both of whom were nodding. "Does that bring us current, gentlemen, or is there any other business for the court?" he asked in a tone that said his boredom threshold had already been exceeded.

"There is, Your Honor. We seek Mrs. Madsen's release *or* bail."

Judge Byers gave a nod and looked to the district attorney. "Mr. Gardner?" he said, making the name sound like a question.

"The people vigorously oppose any request for bail in this case, Your Honor. This is a murder one case." Garrett waited to see what would come next.

"And?" the judge said.

"And, Your Honor, the defendant has committed a violent crime that suggests she presents a danger." The judge stared at him attentively but without expression. "Further, Your Honor, this type of a case presents a serious flight risk if bail is allowed."

Judge Byers furrowed his brow at Garrett. "You believe that Mrs. Madsen presents a danger to society based on what?"

"We are talking about heinous crimes, Your Honor. A shooting at point-blank range," Garrett urged.

"Granted, Mr. Gardner, those are the charges, but wasn't this clearly a crime of passion? Do you have some real reason to believe that Mrs. Madsen will commit a crime if released? Any past record?"

"Your Honor, the state strongly resists bail in any homicide case."

Judge Byers nodded. "Mr. Gardner, the court would appreciate it if we could be a little less generic. Specifically, let me hear you address your concern that Mrs. Madsen is a flight risk. Is there any affirmative evidence that would so indicate?"

Garrett hesitated, clearly not liking the way this was heading. After a lengthy pause, he spoke in a cautious tone, "Not at this time, but as Your Honor knows, such evidence is often hard to come by until after the flight has occurred."

"I do know that, Mr. Gardner. Any specific reason to believe that this defendant might depart the jurisdiction?" the judge pressed.

"The nature of the crime and likely the severe sentence likely to result."

"There is a significant fact assumed in that statement, isn't there, Mr. Gardner? Namely guilt?"

"Yes, Your Honor."

Brian looked at Lloyd, who was smiling now, obviously pleased with the way this was unfolding.

Judge Byers spoke again to Garrett, "Didn't Mrs. Madsen make arrangements to turn herself in to the police?"

"Well, technically, Your Honor. But she really had no choice. We would have picked her up anyway and ..."

Judge Byers smiled sardonically. "I'm sure you would have, Mr. Gardner. But that's my point. You didn't have to."

Garrett drew a breath and then said with renewed self-assurance, "With due respect, Your Honor, I'm not sure that such reasoning should prevail. Suspects who make deals to turn themselves in do so for many reasons known only to them and—" He glanced over at Lloyd and then back to the judge. "Perhaps their counsel. Those reasons, known only to those insiders, are sometimes followed by the suspect fleeing when released on bail."

"Point taken, Mr. Gardner. Speaking in generalities, we both know such cases exist. The court's job is to look at the case before me. In this case, there is no evidence to suggest that Barbara Madsen, who is absent any prior record and who came in of her own accord, presents a substantial flight risk."

"Well, Your Honor, no one would have expected her to have perpetrated a double murder either."

Judge Byers frowned. "And that is not something to be decided or assumed here today. It will be up to a jury to make those decisions, after full consideration of the evidence that has not yet been presented."

"Yes, Your Honor," Garrett said resignedly.

"Assuming that the preliminary hearing presents sufficient evidence to hold the defendant for trial."

Brian blanched at hearing Barbara referred to as "the defendant."

"Well, Your Honor," Garrett offered, preparing to take one more shot at what had become an uphill battle.

Judge Byers interrupted his response by lifting a palm toward him. He nodded to no one in particular, in an apparent nod to the weightiness of what he was about to say. "I'm ready to rule. I do acknowledge the seriousness of the charges presented." He paused and glanced at Barbara. Then he looked alternatively between the lawyers and resumed. "But I do not believe that this defendant presents a danger to society, nor a substantial likelihood of flight risk. Bail is set at five hundred thousand dollars."

He looked at Barbara. "Mrs. Madsen, you are not to leave this city, and you are ordered to appear at the time of the preliminary hearing four weeks from today, at nine o'clock in the morning in this department. Understood?"

Barbara nodded and then said, "Understood, Your Honor."

"If for some reason you do not appear, a warrant will be issued for your arrest, and there will be no further opportunity for bail."

"Understood," Barbara offered once more.

Brian felt a sudden sense of sadness as he saw the hopelessness in her expression.

"And you will face new charges if this court's order is violated in any respect."

"Yes, Your Honor," Barbara said meekly, nodding to convey her intended compliance.

Judge Byers looked to Garrett and then Lloyd and finally said, "Good day, gentlemen. See you in four weeks."

Papers were gathered, and briefcases snapped shut. Brian stood, wanting out of the courtroom before the judge had second thoughts.

They had prepared for bail in advance but had not counted on it in view of Lloyd's repeated warnings that his motion for release on bail may or may not be granted. The bond was posted, and Barbara walked out into the afternoon sunshine within three hours after Judge Byers ruled on the motion.

Lloyd waited with Brian until Barbara emerged in street clothes, in the company of a female sheriff's deputy, who shook Barbara's hand and wished her well before turning to go.

"Thank you, Lloyd," Barbara said softly, extending a hand to him.

Lloyd nodded and took her hand. "I'll get back to you as soon as I have the opportunity to talk further with the DA concerning the specifics of a plea involving counseling and time at a private clinic." He fixed his gaze on Barbara in a way that suggested to Brian he was assessing her mental or emotional state.

She conveyed no emotion but said, "Thank you. I appreciate all you've done." She turned and walked away.

Brian and Lloyd exchanged a look of concern, and Brian followed her.

In the car as Brian drove toward home, Barbara was silent. Her gaze was fixed, seemingly on the road in front of her, but Brian doubted her focus was external.

"You all right?" he asked.

Barbara nodded slowly, remaining silent. After a few moments she spoke, almost in a whisper, "I could get the death penalty, you know?"

Brian recoiled at the words. "No," he said without doubt in his voice. "Lloyd Martin says that won't happen."

As he spoke, he acknowledged to himself that it was a possibility, though an outside one. He looked over at her, but she did not respond. She seemed to be somewhere far away.

When they got home, Barbara excused herself and went upstairs to rest. Brian poured himself a bourbon and water, went into his study, and sat down behind his computer. He struck a few keys and was soon online, searching through recent decisions on Lexis. He called up cases by keying in "murder," "manslaughter," "heat of passion," "mitigation," and "diminished capacity" in California appellate courts.

When the search yielded 143,000 matches, he began to fashion search words to narrow the focus. He knew the process would be a long one, but it was this or sit around and feel helpless. He hoped to find case law to support the diminished capacity plea and favor treatment rather than incarceration. He thought about Barbara's expression as she stared vacantly and sadly into nothingness on the journey back from the courthouse, downed the remainder of his bourbon, and turned his attention back to the monitor and the 6,305 matches generated by his last search. Brian struck at the keyboard as he thought of a way to further narrow his search.

As Brian read excerpts of cases that caught his eye, he noted the prompt return of his ability to analyze cases, a skill that he thought would be stale in the wake of his career change from the practice of law to politics. Just like riding a bicycle, he told himself, as he scanned the head notes of eighty-eight cases in which diminished capacity defenses had been accepted in connection with homicides and batteries in the heat of passion. There had to be something here that would favorably lend itself to analysis of the circumstances under which Barbara had killed Michael Hayward and participated in the killing of Cathy Jenkins.

As he thought again of Barbara's participation in Cathy's murder, a deep chill ran over his spine, followed by a wave of anger. As the moments passed, he realized he was staring into space, and he was shocked to discover that tears were in his eyes. He found himself thinking of Cathy's free spirit and the impromptu trip to the beach in suits on a workday morning. His thoughts suddenly turned to Barbara following them and then to her and Michael Hayward plotting Cathy's killing. He felt a deep and heavy sensation of sadness wash over him, and he leaned back in his chair. He began wringing his hands and closing his eyes tightly. He told himself that he couldn't fall apart. He had to keep going. He pushed the water from his eyes and returned his energy to reading cases. All else would have to wait.

By six in the morning, Brian had found a dozen key cases that he thought would assist Lloyd in making a diminished capacity argument and others that would mitigate in favor of reduced sentences. He had found three times that number that would hurt rather than help, and while he printed all of the cases, he put the negative cases in a different file than the one intended for Lloyd. He would Shepardize the bad ones later, a process used to track the subsequent history of the decisions, in hopes that later appellate cases had reversed or distinguished some of the bad decisions.

Brian picked up the morning paper and scanned for articles about Barbara, himself, Michael Hayward, and Cathy Jenkins, a process that had become a morning ritual. On page two, he found an article "How Tangled the Web—-the Fate of a National Figure." The article recounted the death of Cathy Jenkins, long thought to be a break-in gone wrong, her later suspected relationship with Brian Madsen, and the conspiratorial plans of Barbara Madsen and the now-deceased Michael Hayward, allegedly murdered by his co-conspirator in cold blood.

The article contained quotes from Carol Hayward, grieving spouse and angry victim, seeking justice done against the woman who had murdered her husband. She announced that she would be present at every pretrial motion and hearing and for the full length of the trial. She "lived for" her chance to testify in the sentencing phase of the trial. She expressed anger and regret that Judge Byers had set such a woman free on bail and hoped this judge would not further impede justice.

This woman was ready to fire up a lynch mob, Brian reflected. There was then a reference to a related article examining what it referred to as the now "well-established rights of victims and survivors" to be heard in the sentencing phases of trials and the degree of the loss they describe taken into account by the trial judge to increase the sentence.

There were additional quotes of Carol Hayward and her commitment to testify against Barbara Madsen at every opportunity. The piece concluded with a statement that legal experts believed that the tormented testimony of widows and orphans greatly increased the prosecution's odds of a death penalty result.

"Odds," Brian said aloud, throwing the paper down on the kitchen table.

It was as if these so-called legal experts were speaking of a game of craps rather than someone's life, the latest window in the Vegas sports book. Five to three said she got the death penalty.

Brian rubbed his eyes with the heels of his palms, trying to shake the exhaustion that had a hold of him. The daily articles portraying Barbara as the female counterpart of O. J. Simpson—pathological, slick, and guilty—was poisoning the well of public opinion. The newspapers were actually taking polls from the potential jury pool at large, and 80 percent were leaning toward the death penalty for this total stranger, who had never said a word in her own defense and who would not be permitted to do so by her lawyers. The press was selling newspapers by making her the equivalent of Orwell's Goldstein in *1984*, the root of all evil, the source of all misfortune. Is something going wrong in your life? It probably connects to Barbara Madsen.

Brian spent the next two days turning it over in his mind, frequently returning to thoughts that his straying had done it all, and then forcing himself back on task, racking his brain for something he could do to give Barbara a fighting chance. It suddenly occurred to him that, with a little influence of his own, maybe there was a way to level the playing field. Brian walked to his office and sat down at his desk. He opened his address book, picked up the phone, and punched in the private number of James Francis Orson, friend and confidante to presidents and kings.

On the second ring, it was answered, "Hello."

"Is this Jim Orson?" Brian asked tentatively.

"It is." He cleared his throat and then said, "And this would be Congressman Brian Madsen."

The immediate recognition stunned Brian. He had not spoken to Orson since the inaugural. For a moment, he thought about caller identification, but he blocked caller identification, so the entry should say nothing more than "private caller."

"Hello ... How did you know who it was?" Brian asked awkwardly.

"I have a good memory for faces and voices. Not that I need it. Yours is spread all over the place these days. I know you're not talking to the media about the, shall we say, critical events, but as you are news, the networks have been running every speech and interview you've ever done. Brian Madsen sound bites are everywhere, and your voice is known to everyone who listens to the radio or watches the eleven o'clock news." He paused for a moment and then added, "And I've been figuring that I might hear from you."

"You have?" Brian asked. The surprise was evident in his voice.

"The night of your inaugural wingding, while Sean Gilmore was mugging for the camera, I told you to talk to me if you needed anything. Well ..." He drew out the word as if holding a musical note. "Ain't many folks more in need of help at the moment."

"I see," Brian said, feeling uncomfortably transparent.

"Don't worry though, Congressman. If there's one thing I do well, it's keep a confidence."

"Thank you, Jim. I do appreciate that."

"Now," Orson continued as if Brian hadn't spoken, "if I'm correct—-and you tell me if I am correct—-you would like to know if I can help your wife given her current ..." He paused as if groping for a word. "Situation. Admirable, Congressman. Quite admirable."

Brian was squirming uncomfortably in his chair but said only, "Please call me Brian."

"Right, Brian." Orson drew an audible breath and then said, "This is a hard one, Brian. Influencing the way a criminal prosecution goes down or what sentences are handed out is tough anyway. Particularly so when it's so much in the public eye. These events are selling papers nationally, and it looks like people are going to keep watching this one 'til the fat lady sings. You with me?"

Brian felt deflated and couldn't think of much to say. "Yes, I'm with you. I appreciate you being aware and interested."

He closed his eyes in resignation. "I knew that you probably wouldn't be able to help, but I appreciate your understanding."

"I didn't say there's no way to help, just that it's a tough one. I'll take a run at it and call you later."

"Really?" Brian regained a little hope.

"I'll call you soon," Orson said.

Brian heard a click. He leaned back in his chair and closed his eyes, wondering who Orson would call or what favors he might call in to make something happen. And wouldn't Brian owe him as much or more than any of them if he could make something happen to help Barbara?

Brian opened his eyes, and Barbara was standing in front of him with a faraway look in her eyes. She sat down in one of two chairs on the other side of his desk and looked at him with the eyes of one caught up in sorrow.

Barbara spoke slowly, "I've been thinking that maybe I should go somewhere." She searched his face.

He looked at her in silence, trying to place the statement in context, hoping that she wasn't about to tell him that she was going to skip bail.

She didn't wait for him to speak. "I was thinking maybe Rio De Janeiro, Nicaragua, or Australia."

"Australia?" Brian repeated, focusing on the one that didn't seem to belong. "You know something about those places?"

She nodded. "Some countries aren't as extradition friendly as others. Anyway, I've been doing a little online research, and those are a few that surface as possibilities." It conjured up images of an AOL icon labeled "fugitive favorites."

Barbara continued, "I mean, I may not do it if things go well, but you've seen the papers. I'm as good as convicted."

Brian wasn't sure how to respond. He had seen the papers every day. The walls between them were high, and since all of this, their conversations had been about Barbara's defense or just superficial exchanges. Now she had cut to the chase with one sentence, and he didn't know what to say to her. It struck him that, on some level, he still cared about her and her well-being. It also struck him that he had no thought of loss associated with her possible disappearance. He just wanted to help her, anyway he could.

"You can't do it," he heard himself saying. "How long can you live in hiding? In disguise in some unfamiliar culture? They will get you, and then the chances of parole are gone."

After a few moments of silence, she nodded acknowledgment and then said, "You're probably right. I just feel so trapped. Like a caged animal." She stood up and walked to the door. Then she turned back and looked at him with a smile. "I'll hang on. Thanks for helping me through this. I know you can't love me anymore, and that's really the worst of it all."

Brian could find no words. She stopped and pushed a tear from her eye. "I just wanted to keep you." She didn't wait to see the sadness that overcame his expression, but she quickly turned and walked from the room.

The following morning, Barbara and Brian had coffee together, and Brian told her of the more helpful cases his research had produced. She listened silently, sipping her coffee and occasionally nodding without enthusiasm. As Brian explained a manslaughter result in a case with some similarities, the phone rang.

Barbara ran to pick it up. "Hello," she said with rare enthusiasm. She squeezed the phone tightly. "Yes, Lloyd, I was hoping it was you. What happened?" Her face was alight with anticipation. Over the ensuing moments of silence, he saw the deflation in her expression and then resignation as she stared straight ahead at the wall." After several minutes, she spoke softly, "I see." There was another silence. "Yes, I understand. Thanks." She slowly moved the phone back to its cradle without looking down.

Brian waited, but when she remained quiet, he asked, "What did he say?"

She looked at him and forced a sad smile. "He said no deals. Everything has changed with the DA. Too much publicity and too political. He said they want the death penalty for each of the killings." She shook her head. "What do they want? Do they want to execute me twice?" She walked to the kitchen table and sat down next to him. "I'm really scared," she said, rocking back and forth in the chair.

Brian leaned over and put his arms around her, convinced that his efforts were in vain, as there was no comfort to be found for either of them.

It was ten in the evening when the phone rang, startling Brian. He had been intently studying the Oregon Supreme Court's affirmation of a case that had denied a diminished capacity defense to a woman who had killed her husband. The facts were uncomfortably close.

"Hello," Brian said, his mind still processing the appellate decision.

"Hello, Brian. This is Jim Orson."

The name immediately pulled Brian from his preoccupation. "Jim, hello. Good to hear from you." Brian's heart raced.

"I've been reviewing the problem since we spoke a few days ago," Orson said. "It's going to be very difficult to do much because we have all the wrong elements, including a hungry and political DA, an out-of-control public interest factor, a widow who can hardly wait to testify, the fact that this involves two killings with murder one charges on both, and, as if all that is enough, some pretty good evidence."

"I know, Jim," Brian said. "So are you telling me there's nothing that can be done?"

"No, I'm telling you that there's not much that can be done. I called in a couple of political favors, and I did make some progress."

"What kind of progress?" Brian asked expectantly.

"They won't seek the death penalty. It's going to be turned over to a committee in the DA's office to review the facts and make a recommendation. That recommendation will be carefully considered for about three weeks. Then the committee will recommend that the death penalty not be sought. The committee is not just prosecutors, but some influential private citizens. That keeps the heat of the decision from the DA's office."

There was a silence while Brian assessed, not quite sure of what to say. He wanted to say, "That's it, no death penalty?" Instead he could only say, "I see," reflecting that there was no cause for optimism if a life imprisonment were the best guarantee he could get from a man with Orson's connections.

Orson spoke as if he could read Brian's thoughts. "I know it's not much, Brian," Orson said empathetically, "but I'm afraid it's the best we can do."

"I understand," Brian said softly, "and I appreciate what you've done. Truly. One day—"

Orson didn't let him finish his promise to return the favor. "I just wish we could do more. Keep me informed, Brian. I'll call you if anything else breaks."

Brian found himself wondering who the "we" might be. "Thank you again, Jim. Talk to you soon."

In the first days after Barbara's arrest, Brian had been portrayed as a shady figure who somehow brought about all that had happened in his world and who was unworthy of his position of public trust. The office phones rang off the hook, largely with demands for his resignation or calls for his impeachment. Brian was kept informed but couldn't really bring himself to care. It all had the surreal quality of an out-of-body experience, as if he were watching someone else live this bizarre life and could do nothing but wait for a plot beyond his comprehension to unfold.

As the days passed and details came more into focus, some creative reporter determined that more papers would sell if Brian were a victim rather than a perp. A lengthy article portrayed him as the all-American boy who made good, marrying the girl next door, and then succumbing to the feminine wiles of his own personal Mata Hari. The girl next door and Mata Hari, as it turned out, were one in the same. Brian considered how little the media knew about Barbara, but it didn't stop them from building their own version of her, pouring out pages of details, most of them false or offensive. Then the irony of this thought suddenly struck him. *Just how well had I known Barbara?*

While the image the press manufactured for Barbara angered Brian on a daily basis, the new image created for him turned out to be a salable commodity and presented a bandwagon that the media mainstay could hardly wait to jump aboard.

Suddenly Brian went from a malevolent force loose in the public coffers to the victim of a betrayal fashioned by the woman closest to him in conspiracy with a sociopath. Brian had wondered how Barbara might ever get an untainted jury panel to hear her case. He still wondered whether a fair trial would be possible. The daily dosage of news about the case had become a deluge, and the only potential jury pool would have to be residents of Greenland or comatose.

The calls to Brian's office had suddenly changed, reflecting the new public perception of Brian Madsen. Callers extended condolences, expressed support, and promised to stand by him. Some sent campaign contributions, although he wasn't campaigning for anything. It was thoughtful and caring, and none of it mattered. It was all life after the fall.

Brian's characteristic ambition, drive, and compulsion to somehow make a difference were simply gone. In their place was the abyss—the absence of any reason to get up each day, a sense that every day was less relevant than the last and sucked only a little less than the next would. He was aware that his emotional detachment was a psychological mechanism to keep him from the abyss he stared into daily. So what? This insight was as useless as the day itself.

The dreams Brian had about Cathy had slowly decreased a couple months after her death, and he thought they would fade away. But there had been a recent reversal in those changes, and the dreams were becoming more frequent and more emotionally intense. Now he didn't want to get up in the morning to face the day, and he didn't want to go to bed at night to face the dreams and the rekindling of a better life that he would lose by morning.

In this latest sequence of dreams, Brian had turned the clock back to time they had spent together, had seen the light in her eyes, and had touched her face. Then came the inevitable realization that he would never see her again and he would never have the chance to tell her ... what? That he thought about her, that he missed her, and that life was not the same? And maybe just to talk with her one more time.

Chapter 27

After eight months of failed attempts to negotiate a resolution that would allow Barbara to serve her time in a psychiatric hospital, this was the day it all came to a head. No cameras were to be permitted in the courtroom, but a media circus was surrounding the courthouse. Trailers, satellites, camera operators, miles of cord, and microphones were thrust into the face of any passerby who might share an opinion about Barbara Madsen. Her trial for the murders of both Cathy Jenkins and Michael Hayward had already been carried out in the press, where both evidence and innuendo were admissible and most citizens had already reached a verdict.

Multiple pretrial motions to suppress evidence on Barbara's behalf had been overruled, and all evidence against Barbara would be presented to the jury. As promised, Carol Hayward had been at the preliminary hearing and every motion, appearing anxious for any opportunity to speak.

The trial was estimated to take three weeks, including a parade of witnesses who would testify that Barbara was a wonderful human being, whose perfect record in life before Cathy Jenkins warranted a merciful result. There could be no evidence that suggested Barbara was innocent, as the recorded evidence in Barbara's last conversation with Michael Hayward, was irrefutable. The evidence would instead focus on assertions that these were crimes of passion, worthy of manslaughter convictions only.

According to Lloyd Martin, the best-case scenario was conviction on two counts of manslaughter two, with a total cost to Barbara's life of fifteen years and possible release after ten to twelve with good behavior credit. Thanks to the efforts of Jim Orson and those who moved behind the curtain to obtain the favors that his clout motivated, the worst-case scenario would be a double murder conviction resulting in life imprisonment without possibility of parole.

With Brian's ongoing review of case law, he had come to realize that Orson's accomplishment was no small feat. A second killing was frequently an aggravating factor that elevated a life imprisonment sentence to the death penalty. He owed Orson more gratitude than the disappointment he had conveyed.

Brian parked his car and walked into the court building, took keys and change from his pocket, and put them in a plastic dish. Then he walked through the metal detector. His stomach was in knots, and he wished he could be anywhere else. He emptied the plastic dish into his hand, gave the uniformed guard beside the metal detector a nod, and walked down the hall. Brian took the elevator to the third floor.

He made his way down the corridor until he found the door marked "Department 38" and then checked his watch. Nine fifty-five. He pushed open the door and walked the carpeted aisle toward the front of the courtroom, where a waist-high gate in a wooden barricade separated the participants from the spectators.

As Brian made the walk up the aisle, he noted that the seats on both sides of the aisle were largely unoccupied. There were two dozen men and women, primarily dressed in suits. Some stared at files, while others sat talking. There was no one he recognized, but a number of them looked like members of the press. On the other side of the gated fence were two counsel tables, one of which was occupied by Lloyd Martin and Barbara and the other by Garrett Gardner.

When Brian approached the gate, Lloyd stood and extended a hand as he opened the gate for Brian.

Garrett stood and gave Brian a solemn nod. "Hello, Mr. Madsen," he said and then turned his attention back to the open file on the counsel table in front of him.

Lloyd mumbled a greeting and then pointed a hand to the chair next to his, and Brian sat down.

Brian leaned toward Lloyd and asked, "Where's Barbara? She met with you, right?" It suddenly occurred to Brian that she might have actually had second thoughts and elected to board a plane for Nepal or Ethiopia.

Lloyd said, "Yeah, she just went down the hall."

Brian wasn't sure if he were relieved or if it would have been better for her to be long gone to parts unknown, leaving no clues. He would have understood if she had disappeared, taking her chances on a distant culture rather than fifteen years to natural life in a state prison.

Barbara appeared in the doorway and walked toward them. Her expression was detached and distant. Brian stood and gave her a hug. Then he moved over a chair so she could sit down next to Lloyd.

There was silence for several minutes, at which point the clerk and bailiff entered the room. A moment later the judge emerged from his chambers and stood in the doorway while the bailiff called out, "All rise and come to order, department thirty-eight is now in session, the Honorable James Pierson presiding."

The judge, who appeared to be in his early sixties, was thin-faced, clean-shaven, and bald, except for brief patches of closely cropped gray above each ear. He walked rapidly to the bench and sat down, the clerk's cue to turn to the thin crowd and announce, "You may be seated."

They sat down and waited expectantly while the judge reviewed documents in front of him and then looked from one counsel table to the other over his glasses. "Are the parties ready to proceed in connection with the matter of the people versus Barbara Madsen?"

Both attorneys stood. Then Garrett said, "Garrett Gardner for the people, Your Honor. We are ready to proceed."

Lloyd responded, "Lloyd Martin for Ms. Madsen, Your Honor. We are also ready."

"Fine," Pierson said. "Who wants to go first?"

Garrett spoke up, "Your Honor, the state first moves for dismissal of the charges in connection with case number 1931781."

"That would be all charges in connection with the death of Catherine Jenkins?" Judge Pierson asked.

"Correct, Your Honor," Garrett said.

"And the reason?" Pierson probed.

"Lack of sufficient evidence, Your Honor."

Pierson furrowed his brow. "As I recall, we had a preliminary hearing in connection with this case. And Judge ... " He paused for a moment as he reviewed the file in front of him. "Constance Mathews of the municipal court found that there was sufficient evidence for this matter to proceed to trial. Is that correct, Mr. Gardner?"

"It is, You Honor. The reason for the dismissal has arisen in the investigation and analysis of the evidence since the prelim," Garrett said with apparent confidence. Pierson didn't look convinced, so Garrett spoke again. "The dismissal has been approved all the way up to the district attorney, Your Honor."

Pierson furrowed his brow and nodded, seemingly appeased yet curious. "Seems a little strange given the findings of the municipal court and the magnitude of this case." He directed the comment to Garrett, who remained quiet. Pierson then looked to Lloyd. "Okay with you, I presume, Mr. Martin?"

"Yes, Your Honor. I was informed of these developments late yesterday, and I have no objection to the dismissal."

Pierson issued a sardonic smile. "I would think not, Mr. Martin. I would think not. If I were the district attorney, however, I would have many questions." He leaned back in his chair and grinned widely. "And given the scope of the press coverage in this case, I suspect that he'll have many to answer." He nodded to no one in particular and then said, "All charges against this defendant in connection with the death of Catherine Jenkins are hereby dismissed."

He read the case number for the benefit of the court record and then looked back to the parties. "Next order of business. My clerk tells me that you have a proposed plea bargain in connection with the matter."

Brian looked at Lloyd expectantly, as this was news to him.

"That's correct. We have worked out the details this morning." He glanced down at Brian with what looked like an apologetic expression for not having divulged this development. Then he turned his attention back to the judge.

Brian was stunned. He was the true outsider with no knowledge that any deal had been achieved or even seriously contemplated.

"Mr. Gardner?" the judge inquired.

"Yes, Your Honor, we have reached agreed recommendations for the court."

"Very well," the judge said. "Enlighten me."

Garrett deferred to Lloyd with a wave in his direction.

Lloyd cleared his throat and began, "The parties have agreed that Barbara Madsen will plead no lo contendre to manslaughter two in connection with the death of Michael Hayward, Your Honor. Sentencing recommendations have been included in the stipulations filed with the court."

His Honor nodded silently for a moment. He then spoke directly to Barbara, "Is it your desire, Ms. Madsen, to enter into the plea agreement voiced by Mr. Martin?"

Barbara stood and said, "It is, Your Honor."

"And you do so voluntarily and of your own free will without coercion from any source?"

"That's right, Your Honor," Barbara replied.

"Do you understand, Ms. Madsen, that, in pleading in this manner, you are waiving your right to any trial by judge or jury?"

Barbara nodded. "Yes, sir. I do."

"Do you understand that you are also waiving rights of appeal in connection with your plea?"

"Yes, sir," Barbara said without hesitation.

The judge removed his glasses and looked at Barbara intently, as if he could see her more clearly without them. "You are aware that sentencing recommendations have been made?"

"Yes, sir."

"Have you also been made aware that I am not compelled to accept those recommendations? That they are only recommendations and that, if the court deems appropriate, they may be entirely disregarded, and sentencing will made in accordance with statute?"

"Yes, sir."

Brian leaned toward Lloyd and whispered, "Maybe she should reconsider. Does that mean he's going to let her have it with both barrels?"

Lloyd shook his head and waved off Brian. When Brian looked up, he saw the judge was watching him.

"Do we have a question here?" Pierson asked.

"No, Your Honor, we're good," Lloyd replied.

Brian began to speak, but Lloyd again shook his head, so Brian yielded. This was, after all, Lloyd's battlefield.

"I'm told we are prepared to waive time and proceed with sentencing today. Is that right, counsel?"

"Yes, Your Honor," Lloyd and Garrett said almost in one voice.

"Very well." The judge paused and scanned the courtroom. "If family of Michael Hayward is present and would like to be heard, please stand to be identified."

Brian knew this was a relatively new requirement of state law that required the court to allow the victim's family to be heard and to take the testimony of a victim's family into account before making a sentencing decision. Although the law presented a singular opportunity for relatives to confront a perpetrator and was probably of psychological benefit to those venting, in a legal sense, it seemed of dubious value. Relatives of the deceased were always distraught, and even if they weren't, why should the penalty be stiffer because the victim was liked more by his relatives? If you killed someone, he or she was no less dead because there was a rift between family members.

In this case, the point was moot. Brian looked around the courtroom and was surprised to see no one come forward. He remembered Carol Hayward, besieged by grief, expressing through tears to clambering reporters that she would be present in court to seek justice against her husband's killer and to maximize the sentence Barbara would receive for ending his life and their lives together. The woman seemed to be living for this day. *How could she not be present?*

Brian scanned the courtroom one more time. The eyes of the onlookers did the same, but no one stood.

Apparently, Judge Pierson read the same newspapers as everyone else and was aware of Carol Hayward's vows to testify because his eyes scanned the room a second time, and his expression registered surprise when there was no response. When the judge had satisfied himself that there were no takers, he gave a nod and looked toward the reporter.

"For the record, no one has come forward to be heard."

She nodded acknowledgment, but like all court reporters, she didn't want to speak, or she would have to record her own words as well as everyone else's.

Judge Pierson looked at Barbara, and all eyes focused on him as he spoke, "Barbara Madsen, the court will accept your plea. There can be no doubt that the crime in this case was more than serious. It was brutal, heinous, and, to most, unimaginable."

Brian grabbed Lloyd's arm involuntarily. This judge was going to ignore whatever guidelines had been agreed and put away Barbara forever, and there was not a damn thing he or any of them could do about it.

Judge Pierson continued with his eyes never leaving Barbara's. "Nonetheless, it was a crime of passion in the heat of an unplanned moment. This is not any form of justification, but it does mitigate in favor of more moderate sentencing. Accordingly, this court will accept the sentencing proposal advanced by the parties. Barbara Madsen, please rise."

Barbara and Lloyd both stood, assumed a submissive posture, and waited for Judge Pierson to continue. "You are hereby sentenced to seven years in the California Institute for Women. You are remanded to the custody of the county sheriff for transport."

"Your Honor," Lloyd said in the first moment of silence, "we had requested that Mrs. Madsen be given seven days to put things in order and handle family matters before reporting to begin serving her sentence."

Judge Pierson look momentarily annoyed, as if he had caught Lloyd engaging in an act of overreaching. He looked at Garrett. "Any response from the people?"

Garrett paused a little too long and then said, "We would have no problem with forty-eight hours, Your Honor."

The judge's expression reflected annoyance. "Two days is okay, but seven is too long, counsel."

Garrett was having second thoughts. "Perhaps it would be better if there were no delay." But it was stated without conviction, and it seemed that Garrett was aware this argument was too late in coming.

Judge Pierson looked at Barbara. "For the same reasons you were granted bail originally, you will have seventy-two hours from right now to report. That means Thursday at noon. During that seventy-two-hour period, you will not leave the city. The bond previously posted will remain in effect until your return. Are we clear? Any questions?"

"We are clear. Thank you, Your Honor," Barbara said responsively.

Lloyd nodded his concurrence.

Judge Pierson stood and then stated, "This court is in recess for fifteen minutes."

Everyone stood as Judge Pierson walked from the bench to his chambers, opened the door, and disappeared from view. The buzz of voices filled the room, while some of the reporters ran for the door. Others waited, poised to talk to any of the key characters in the day's drama, in hopes of bagging a spot on the eleven o'clock news.

Brian looked at Lloyd, who was smiling. "Is that what was agreed?" Brian asked incredulously. "Seven years in a state penitentiary?"

Lloyd nodded, still smiling. "Sort of. The Institute is a minimum-security facility. As in no fences. It has dorms, televisions, and the opportunity to work or study. With good behavior credit, Barbara will be out in forty-eight to fifty-four months."

Brian considered all this. It was delivered as if forty-eight to fifty-four months would conclude right after lunch. When Brian last checked, this was four to four and a half years. He looked at Barbara, who was nodding at something Lloyd had said and seemed to be taking all this well.

The court attendant, a pretty Hispanic woman of about thirty, who wore a red jacket that made her look like a realtor, motioned toward Lloyd, who nodded and led Barbara and Brian through a side door in the courtroom into a hallway. She motioned down the hall toward the interior elevators.

Lloyd smiled at her. "Thanks. I appreciate you getting us out of there before the swarm had us cornered."

"My pleasure," she said, pointing down the hallway, "but I'd get out of here as soon as possible if I were you. It won't be long before they make it to the side door."

They followed Lloyd down the hallway and entered an open elevator. Walking quickly, they reached the third floor of the parking structure without being discovered.

"Thank you, Lloyd," Barbara said, giving him a hug.

Lloyd nodded. "Let's meet at my office on Thursday morning, and I'll come back with you. Let's say eleven thirty?"

Barbara nodded. "Okay, I'll see you then."

Brian mumbled some additional thanks to Lloyd, who smiled and then turned to walk in the direction of his car.

In silence, Brian drove Barbara a few rows away to where she was parked. She climbed out, stopping before closing the door and looking in at him.

"Take me to lunch at Rosie's, and I'll talk to you about all this. I'm yearning for something familiar."

Brian smiled weakly and nodded. She closed the door and climbed into her Chrysler. Then she followed him from the parking structure. As Brian drove the familiar streets of the neighborhood he had known for years toward Rosie's Diner, everything looked the same but felt uncomfortably different.

Brian and Barbara parked and walked into Rosie's, where the lunchtime crowd was thinning, and a young girl who wore a "hostess" badge told them that a table would be ready in just a moment.

As they stood in the lobby, Brian asked, "When did you know about the deal?"

"Just this morning. About fifteen minutes before you arrived."

Brian found himself feeling relieved for her. "Five years ... maybe four," he said, thinking aloud. He furrowed his brow. "But why were the charges dismissed in connection with one of the deaths?"

"I don't know," she said, shaking her head. "Lloyd didn't either. He didn't want to ask. The whole gift horse thing, I guess."

Brian nodded. "What about Carol Hayward? I can't figure why she was a no-show."

Barbara shrugged. "No idea. I think everyone was shocked."

The young hostess led them to a booth by the window and then disappeared. They sat silently for a few moments and then ordered burgers and Cokes from a server wearing a pink top and a poodle skirt, who received the orders with a nod but wrote nothing.

As the server turned and walked away, Barbara's eyes were fixed on Brian. "I want you to know how grateful I am, Brian, for everything." He started to shake his head, but she held up a hand in a halting motion. "I mean it, Brian. You don't know how close I've come ..." She let the words trail off, turning her head to the window. Then she drew a deep breath and looked back at him.

"It's all right." Brian touched her hand. "I'm glad you made the plea agreement," he said softly. "I can't bear to think of you spending the rest of your life ..."

She smiled and then said, "Thank you for everything." The smile left her face. "I can't stay, Brian. I'm not going to prison."

"What? I figured with this result ..." He let the words trail off. Brian could hardly process the information. There was a whirlwind of feeling he couldn't voice. As he sat silently with her eyes searching his, he had no idea what he wanted to tell her.

She smiled. "Don't worry. I'll be all right." She glanced around the restaurant before speaking further. Then her eyes returned to his. "But I need one more favor."

Brian nodded. "What do you need?"

"Time. I need the next ... " She checked her watch. "Sixty-five hours until we're supposed to meet at Lloyd's office. Then you can tell them I went to the grocery store and never returned or whatever you want."

"Are you sure?" he asked reflectively. "Maybe four or five years ..."

"I'm sure," she said confidently. "I've been thinking about little else."

He nodded.

"I'm leaving from here. I packed what I needed yesterday, and it's in the car." She clasped her hands together and leaned toward him. "There will be lots of questions, and I'm sorry for that. But you won't know where I've gone or who I'll be, so you won't have any information to give."

Brian searched her face for more. They were both silent as she stood. "I'm going to the restroom." She smiled warmly. "Did you remember this place has a backdoor near the ladies' room?"

"Will I see you again?" Brian asked, knowing the answer.

"Maybe a postcard. Anonymously, of course." She kissed him on the cheek. "Take care, lover. I'll miss you." She forced a smile and touched his cheek. "Find a way to start over." She turned away from the table, and he watched her walk away and disappear down the hall toward the restroom.

The poodle-skirted server returned and put the burgers on the table. "Want any more soda?"

Brian shook his head. "No, thanks."

The server pointed toward the restroom. "How about your wife? You think she wants more?"

Brian smiled at the woman. "No, I don't think she does."

Chapter 28

When Brian paid the check and left Rosie's, it was just after one in the afternoon. As Brian walked out into the sunshine, his stomach was churning, and his emotions were in turmoil. He drove out of the parking lot and down the street to the freeway.

Brian drove for almost an hour, moving from one freeway to another with no destination. His thoughts traveled through snapshots of his years with Barbara—their first kiss, passionate and wonderful, and the first house they bought together, a fixer-upper they couldn't afford. It struck him that more recent memories were fewer and lacked the same passion. He replayed the scene as Barbara walked away from the table at Rosie's and considered that he might never see her again.

On impulse, Brian got off the freeway and found himself in a residential suburb of well-manicured homes that was entirely unfamiliar. There was comfort in the unfamiliar. He parked the car and began walking. As he walked, he thought about the early years, when he and Barbara had nothing but innocence and had been so happy. Brian wondered exactly when their love had slipped away, but he couldn't remember. He knew he had not been in love with Barbara for a long time, but even after the love was gone, they shared the remembrance of laughter, tears and fears, intimate moments, sacred feelings, and hard times. It was a bond that they could keep when everything else was gone, at least until he met Cathy and all of their lives unraveled. Brian wondered if Barbara were tormented by what she had done. Through it all, she had never expressed remorse, nor even mentioned the two people who had died at her hand, other than in the context of her own defense. He considered that she would spend her life until she was caught with no personal freedom, getting close to no one and just surviving the days. It sounded so hopeless. Then it occurred to him that his life would not be much different.

At five o'clock, Brian arrived home after two hours of walking. He unlocked the front door of the house and walked inside. Most of Barbara's personal effects were still there, but it felt different. It was too quiet, as if the house kept a secret. He threw his suit jacket across the arm of the couch and made his way to the wet bar in the living room, poured himself a bourbon, and stared out the window to the street. Kids played football in the street with passing cars making their way home frequently interrupting the game. The sky to the west had turned golden to form the beginnings of sunset.

He heard a sound, a squeak, the movement of a door from somewhere behind him. It had come from down the hallway. He turned, remained completely still, and listened, but he heard nothing. Slowly and silently, Brian began making his way down the hallway. He glanced in the guest room. It was empty. He opened the bathroom door and looked inside. *Nothing.*

He continued walking down the hall toward the master bedroom. When he was within ten feet of the door, a figure emerged from the bedroom, stopped in the hall, and stared at him. Brian felt his knees buckle and give way. Then he grabbed and held tight to the wall. He closed his eyes and shook his head in an attempt to clear the impossible image. When he opened his eyes, he saw that it had not moved. It was an apparition.

The apparition stared back at him, now smiling. "Hello, Brian."

He took an involuntary step backward. His ears and eyes were now deceiving him. There was no mistaking who stood before him. "Cathy?"

She nodded. "Yes, it's really me."

Brian studied her, not sure what to believe. She wore jeans and a gray sweater. Her hair was as it had been the night he last saw her. Her face had the same beautiful contour he remembered, and if there were more light, he was sure her eyes would be as blue. He caught sight of an object in her right hand, a bloody towel. He looked from the towel back to her eyes, still not moving.

She looked down and then at the blood-stained towel. "I cut myself getting into the house through your laundry room window. I came in through the backyard. It wouldn't do for anyone to see me. You've been watched, and I'm dead."

Brian stared in disbelief. "Is it really you?"

The smile that he remembered and now dreamed about flooded her face. She ran to him and threw her arms around him. They each held tightly to the other, as if fending off a recurrence of her disappearance. Brian said nothing for several minutes, lost in the embrace and the sights and smells of her. It was just as it had been, just as he had prayed it would be. It was his chance to hold her and to tell her how he felt. It was an opportunity to look in those eyes again. But now there were questions that made their way into his thoughts, inquiries that had to be answered.

He pulled back from her and looked into her eyes. Thoughts spun wildly, and he tried to figure out where to begin. There was expectation in her eyes. "You were dead. It was on the news. At first I hoped it wasn't true, but it was confirmed. Medically. And—"

"And by positive identification of next of kin," she said, finishing the thought.

Brian nodded slowly, remembering. He felt a chill pass through him as his thoughts moved to the images of the death scene. He felt a surge of anger rise up in him as he momentarily relived what it had been like to live through her death.

"So you lied. This was all some damn scam or something."

Her eyes filled with sadness as she spoke. "I never planned any of this. It all just happened." She paused, and Brian saw her watching his eyes. "Can we go sit down somewhere?"

Brian stared at her for a few moments, searching for a clue. Then he nodded. He turned and led the way to the family room. She sat down on the couch, and he fixed them a drink. He handed her the glass and then sat in the armchair across the coffee table from her.

"So what happened? You obviously aren't dead."

She looked down at her lap and nodded. "I made a mistake, Brian. I want you to know that I'm not proud of what got this all started."

"Go on," he said, prompting.

"About two weeks before the night it happened, the feelings started, and within a few days after that, I knew instinctively that it was true. You were getting ready to say good-bye to me." She forced a smile but didn't wait for confirmation from Brian. "I tried to get used to the idea. I told myself that I was quite capable of being alone. I had always been independent."

She closed her eyes as she reflected. Then she opened them and looked at Brian. "But I was lying to myself, and I knew it. I was madly and completely in love with you. I just couldn't watch you go. I was the stereotypical other woman, head over heels, slowly convincing myself that we were the real thing and you knew it too. That you would leave her to be with me."

She shook her head as she reflected. "Then I started to see it in your eyes. You were some uncomfortable combination of restrained and anxious. You were looking for a way to tell me it was over, and more than anything in the world, I didn't want that to happen. That's why, when Michael Hayward came to talk to me, I listened. At first I thought he was crazy. But between his logic and my desperation ..." She let the words trail off.

Brian was incredulous. "Michael Hayward came to you? With what?"

"With a plan. I disappear for a while without explanation. No ransom. No contact. Hayward spearheads a company-sponsored search for the missing executive. And you miss me and worry about me. When the time is right, he gets an anonymous tip as to my whereabouts and gives it to you. You come find me, and we find each other forever." She shook her head. "I know it sounds crazy now. In retrospect, it does to me too. Then it actually sounded like it might work."

Brian's head was pounding. "And what was Hayward going to get out of all this?"

She took a deep breath. "Jason Ross. I had the goods on Jason Ross. A little insider trading. I was supposed to let out that information through an anonymous source when I came back. That's why I thought this was on the up and up. I knew that Hayward really wanted Jason Ross."

She put her elbows on her knees and cupped her face in her hands. When she looked back at Brian, there was a tear in her eye. "You have to know, Brian. I had no idea he meant to blackmail you to kill Jason."

Brian nodded. "I believe you, but you didn't disappear. You died, or we all thought you did."

"Believe me, I was as surprised as anybody. I saw the whole thing on the news. My death. Reports of my funeral. It was unbelievable."

Brian felt the anger rising. "Then why didn't you come forward? Why didn't you do something about it? Why didn't you put a stop to Hayward's insanity? You were the only one who could have."

Cathy took a deep breath. "Can we get out of this hallway?"

Brian was slow to respond. Then he nodded and led the way into the family room. In the greater light of the room, her eyes shone as they always had.

Cathy walked to the picture window that looked out to the backyard. "I've wondered for so long how I would tell you when the day came. I've practiced a thousand times and had nightmares about your reaction a thousand more."

Both were quiet. Then with her back to Brian, she spoke again, "I couldn't come forward because he made me stay dead." She pivoted and looked at him with pained eyes. "He had my family too. You remember how they identified the body? I mean, confirmed it was me who had been beaten to a pulp?"

Brian thought for a moment. "Your sister identified the body. Linda?"

"That's right."

"Yes," Brian reflected, "but why would she do that?"

"Hayward did his homework. Linda was the beneficiary of my life insurance policy, and somehow he knew it. Half a million dollars. People have been killed for a lot less. And someone purporting to be me died in my place that day, remember? I left my apartment in the middle of the night to become missing for a while, as Hayward had planned. Next thing I know, the police are hauling a dead body they think is me out of my apartment. And why wouldn't they? She meets the description, although there's not much left of her face. She's in my apartment, wearing my clothes and has a couple of my wisdom teeth in her mouth. My dentist's records would confirm that he took only two of the four. Linda confirms the identification, and I'm pronounced dead."

Brian watched the distress on her face as she relived the story.

"Then Hayward contacted me. He said that, if I appeared or if I said anything to anybody, my sister would be identified as perpetrating an insurance fraud. And to make sure he had my attention, he told me that, before the dust settled from her criminal activities, she would suddenly die." The glass she held began to shake in her hand.

"As he put it, it would be a real family tragedy with both sisters dead."

"Jesus," Brian said. Brian walked over and took the glass from her. She hugged herself, as if she were chilled. Then he wrapped his arms around her.

"I don't know," she said softly. "I haven't really felt okay since all this began."

Brian helped her sit on the couch. Then he sat down next to her. He looked at her questioningly. "Dental records," he said suddenly. "They matched your dental records to the victim. I remember because that news extinguished my last hope that it wasn't you."

She nodded. "You're right. He was so fucking smart," she responded with anger in her voice. "I had told him that I was having problems with my two remaining wisdom teeth and I wanted to go to the dentist. He told me that he had a dentist friend who would do it right away. I didn't want to change dentists, but he convinced me that his man was good and we had to act fast. His dentist friend took both wisdom teeth the day I disappeared. They wound up in her mouth."

Brian felt nauseated. He looked at Cathy solemnly and asked, "Who died that day?"

"Jackie Carlisle. She was a secretary who worked at the company and was thought to have had a long-term affair with Michael Hayward. He had broken it off, and she was unhappy. Starting to say things around the company about him. About going to his wife. I even heard a few rumblings about him having plans for vengeance against Jason Ross. So she died as me, after leaving a note to friends and family that she was depressed and planned to start over somewhere else. I don't know how he got her to write that note, but the man could get people to do anything. When he was done, it was the perfect murder. The supposed victim had left town, and Michael Hayward had no motive to kill the person everyone believed was dead. Then he takes it even further by blackmailing you. He would send you to jail for killing me unless you killed someone else. It was all brilliantly insane."

Cathy stared at the wall behind Brian, immersed in thought. She spoke with fear in her voice. "He even convinced Barbara that she was a party to killing me. The only thing he never planned was that his arrogance would anger her enough to point a gun at him and pull the trigger." Cathy looked at Brian empathetically. "I'm so sorry you had to go through all this. You were so innocent and didn't deserve any of this."

"What?" Brian responded. The shock was evident. "Innocent? My straying caused all of this."

Cathy's expression suggested that she had been kicked in the stomach. "Is that what we did? Strayed?" She looked away and then back to his eyes. "I'm so sorry if that's what it was for you." Her voice broke. "I had never been so much in love in my life. To me you were—and are—the one." She turned away her head and fought back a tear.

Both were silent for a time. All of this was swimming around in Brian's mind, new pieces in what had been a hopeless puzzle. Suddenly he heard himself say, "You knew that Barbara was being charged in the murders. You silently let her go to trial and maybe suffer the death penalty for killing you?"

Cathy forced a smile in the face of his anger. "Did I?"

Brian stared at her, perplexed. He was no longer sure of anything.

She asked, "Did Barbara ultimately face two counts of murder?"

Brian was stunned one more time. Words eluded him, and all he could say was, "No, she didn't."

"I couldn't announce I was alive without endangering my family, but I had to do something so I moved around behind the curtain. Turns out purgatory really does exist. I appeared to the assistant district attorney one night at his house in Pasadena. I left him a fingerprint. After he verified that I was who I said I was, we made a deal. Charges against Barbara Madsen in connection with my prematurely announced death get dismissed, or I go public and make sure they look like assholes. Turns out his boss wants to run for the Senate, so he can't afford to look like an asshole. I suggested to them that they make sure that a deal is struck with your wife where she doesn't do any more time than anyone would for killing an insane scumbag in the heat of passion."

She shook her head. "These guys were so caught up in the politics that they wouldn't acknowledge that someone else must have died, so no one will investigate the real murder. Jackie Carlisle is still just out of town, even though they know better."

"You did that?" Brian asked. "You got Barbara the deal." The question was rhetorical, but gratitude was in his voice. "It's amazing. Thank you for helping her." This time his voice broke as he held back the emotion.

"Does anyone else know you're still alive?" Brian asked.

"Just two others. I went to visit Carol Hayward. She was stubborn and angry. When I first encouraged her not to testify against Barbara, she was going to call the cops and have me arrested for blackmail and obstruction of justice."

Brian thought of the venom of her quotes against Barbara and how she seemed to be living for the opportunity to avenge her husband's death with her testimony. "You changed her mind," he said, more as a statement than a question.

"She and I stayed up all night drinking tea and talking about the wealth of things that would blacken her husband's memory if it were known that I was alive and I was forced to testify. By morning, we agreed that I would stay dead, and she no longer had any testimony to give."

"Damn," Brian said, "you are amazing."

She forced a smile.

"You said there were two others who knew you were alive. Who's the other one?"

"Barbara," she said softly. And Brian almost fell off his seat.

"You met with Barbara?"

"I wouldn't say we met. I helped her online anonymously. I also did a little research for her on the subject of extradition and pointed her in the right direction when she was looking for a couple of contacts in unknown places. Mostly she was scared."

"You know where she went?" Brian asked, astonished.

She nodded. "Yeah, but I'm no threat. I'm dead, remember?"

"I owe you so much," Brian said, touching her hand.

She shook her head. "No, you don't. I was part of the problem and wanted to be able to go on living with myself. I did what I had to do." She looked gravely off into space. When she spoke again, it was with sadness in her voice. "Gratitude is not something I want from you, Brian."

Cathy stood up and looked around. "Best I disappear the way I came." She looked toward the backdoor.

"Well, wait," Brian said, standing. A sense of desperation came over him. "Where are you staying? How can I find you?"

She smiled. "I've been living in a suburb of London called Barnett. I got a job as a marketing director for a public relations company. I had to take some time off to come back here and move around like a shadow, but I really think I'm on the way to starting over."

"Is there a number in case something comes up?" he asked.

She smiled and then walked over and kissed him softly. "Good-bye, Brian. I hope you won't hate me for what I've done. I'm so sorry." She walked to the backdoor and then turned to look at him. "Have a good life, Brian." She turned and walked out the door, closing it behind her.

Brian sat down at the kitchen table. All of it made sense—the intricate plans of a madman, the undoing of everyone he touched, Cathy's movement behind the scenes to produce what had been unexplainable dismissal of charges for the murder of Cathy Jenkins, the sudden deal for a lenient sentence, and the non-appearance of a witness dedicated to burying Barbara.

Brian felt a sudden emptiness when Cathy had walked out the backdoor. He tried to recapture her words. She had said that she was madly and completely in love with him. But that was then. He thought about the look on her face as she had spoken the words. She still loved him.

"What else did she say?" he said aloud. "Gratitude is not what I want from you."

But there was something she had wanted. And she had been deeply disappointed when he had spoken of their relationship as his "straying." He thought of his dreams of her when she came back to him.

Brian found himself with a foreboding feeling, a sensation that he had just made a terrible mistake. She had come back into his life, and he had let her get away again. Not dead, but gone from his life with a parting wish that he have a good life. He found himself feeling quietly desperate. And the revelation was complete.

Brian called the airlines and made a reservation for a flight to London on the red-eye. *What was the name of the town? Berkeley? No, Barnett. That was it*, he thought. He would make a hotel reservation on the way to the airport. He would be on the way to regaining his life with the woman he loved. He would come back to his role in the Senate, but only if Cathy were prepared to return with him. Otherwise, he would mail in his resignation and become a barrister or open a pub. He would practice dropping the letter "h" from the beginning of his words and driving on the left side of the road, and he would do it all with Cathy by his side.

Chapter 29

Brian looked in the mirror as he walked through the lobby of the mansion. His hair was all gray now, but it served to enhance his image as the elder statesman. He walked into the ballroom where the who's who of national politics schmoozed, toasted, danced, and celebrated in accustomed black-tie. Balloons drifted overhead, and the orchestra played an old Glenn Miller tune. The faces had changed, but the room was timeless.

Brian strode up to the microphone, and the band stopped playing. "Hello, my friends," he said to an outpouring of applause. "I want to thank you for coming out to celebrate the welcoming of a great teammate. I have the honor of introducing California's new junior Congressman to the fold. I have been proud to count his late father among my closest friends for the entire twenty-five years I have had the pleasure of serving in office. Please welcome Francis Orson Jr., an accomplished lawyer with a brilliant career ahead of him. You'll want to be good to Frank because he will succeed us old-timers one day."

Brian raised his glass. "A toast to California's newest treasure. Frank, come on up." Brian hugged Frank Orson and handed him the microphone.

"Thank you, Brian Madsen, from me and on behalf of the people of the State of California. My father counted you among his closest friends also. I'm convinced that there were things between the two of you over these years that he never shared, but I know how much he valued you and your friendship. I am privileged to have you as a mentor as I enter Congress, and the people are privileged to have had you looking out for them for twenty-five years, with many more to come."

Applause filled the room and then gradually faded. A large group crowded around Orson, and the music resumed.

As Brian looked on, he heard a loving voice at his side. "His big night," she said, taking his hand.

"Yes, it is. And he's right about how wonderful the last twenty-five years have been. But the best part of those years has been you."

She squeezed his hand affectionately. "You remember the night of your inaugural?"

He looked over at her and grinned. She wore a strapless blue dress and a single strand of white pearls. As they always had, her blue eyes drew him in and held him.

"How could I forget," he said, smiling. "It changed my life."

Cathy Madsen kissed him on the cheek. "I love you, Brian," she whispered. "It would be just as wonderful today."

"It will be even better." He took her hand, and they walked up the marble staircase toward the bathroom down the hall.

Dear reader,

We hope you enjoyed reading *Sealing Fate*. Please take a moment to leave a review, even if it's a short one. Your opinion is important to us.

Discover more books by David P. Warren at
https://www.nextchapter.pub/authors/author-david-warren

Want to know when one of our books is free or discounted? Join the newsletter at http://eepurl.com/bqqB3H

Best regards,

David P. Warren and the Next Chapter Team

You might also like:
The Whistleblower Onslaught by David P. Warren

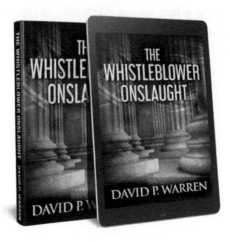

To read the first chapter for free, head to:
https://www.nextchapter.pub/books/the-whistleblower-onslaught

About the Author

David P. Warren is an experienced attorney, mediator and arbitrator. He has represented many clients in employment and business litigation and draws on his experiences to provide a suspenseful thriller that centers on politics, business, ambition and betrayal. David has a passion for storytelling, for characters, and for plot twists and turns that keep the reader spellbound. Sealing Fate is David's first novel and one you will not forget. He introduces you to successful attorney and new Congressman Brian Madsen, whose life is about to be forever altered by an affair, a murder and blackmail.

David has since written 'Altering Destiny,' the story of Lynn Kelly's life on the run after finding money and proof of crimes. His newest book is 'The Whistleblower Onslaught,' in which employment attorney Scott Winslow has his life turned upside down when he takes on a whistleblower case against an energy company. Each is a page-turner you won't want to put down.

Lightning Source UK Ltd.
Milton Keynes UK
UKHW022223050221
378341UK00011B/565/J